She stopped the car and stared at the small white slab of concrete.

It looked so insignificant. Water gushed across the top, but she'd crossed deeper mud holes in this car so she wasn't worried. Not about the water.

Was she about to cross over to another dimension, another life completely? Give up her hard-won independence and be governed again by her family's needs? She'd driven all the way from California, concentrating on the road trip and avoiding the thought of the end of her journey. But once she drove across that bridge there would be no turning back.

Who was she kidding? There'd been no turning back since she'd discovered Gram needed her.

CHRISTINE LYNXWILER and her husband, Kevin, live in the foothills of the beautiful Ozark Mountains in their home state of Arkansas. Christine's greatest earthly joy is her family and aside from God's work, spending time with them is her top priority. She has written three novellas for Barbour anthologies, the most current one being "My True Love Gave to Me," included in the *All Jingled Out* and *Simply Christmas* anthologies.

HEARTSONG PRESENTS

Books by Christine Lynxwiler
HP526—In Search of Love
HP 549—Patchwork and Politics
HP 609—Through the Fire

Don't miss out on any of our super romances. Write to us at the following address for information on our newest releases and club information.

Heartsong Presents Readers' Service
PO Box 719
Uhrichsville, OH 44683

Or visit www.heartsongpresents.com

Longing for Home

Christine Lynxwiler

Heartsong Presents

Dedicated to my sister, Jan Reynolds, who went above and beyond the call of duty to help me meet my deadline. And to my other sisters—Sandy Gaskin, Lynda Sampson, and Vicky Daughety. I'll always remember our all-night plotting session.

Thanks to Tracey Bateman, Lynette Sowell, Annalisa Daughety, Susan Downs, and Susan May Warren for critiquing parts or all of this for me. Thanks to my husband, Kevin, for being incredibly patient and understanding. I love you.

A note from the Author:
I love to hear from my readers! You may correspond with me by writing:

Christine Lynxwiler
Author Relations
PO Box 719
Uhrichsville, OH 44683

ISBN 1-59310-492-8

LONGING FOR HOME

Our mission is to publish and distribute inspirational products offering exceptional value and biblical encouragement to the masses.

All scripture quotations are taken from the King James Version of the Bible.

All of the characters and events in this book are fictitious. Any resemblance to actual persons, living or dead, or to actual events is purely coincidental.

PRINTED IN THE U.S.A.

Or check out our Web site at www.heartsongpresents.com

prologue

Seventeen-year-old Brandi Delaney paused at the top of the stairs. Jake McFadden had his back to her, but she could imagine his dark blue eyes and flashing dimples. She'd been surprised when he'd called and asked her to go with him to Dana's party. In addition to the fact that he was the cutest guy in the senior class, she could think of another really good reason to say yes.

Just last week Jake and Tammy Roland had called it quits. The word in the halls was that he'd done the dumping. Which meant Tammy—who had personally appointed herself as Brandi's tormentor—would be furious when she saw them together. Brandi hated to admit it, but she could hardly wait.

"Hey, Jake. Sorry I wasn't down here to let you in." She stepped off the bottom stair and smiled.

Jake spun around. His grin began slowly and spread across his face. Even though she'd only known him as part of the "in" crowd, she loved that grin.

"Hi. No problem." He chuckled. "Valerie let me in. I guess she's your little sister?"

Brandi groaned. "Yeah." She tucked her hair behind her ear.

He smiled. "Well, if she ever gets tired of elementary school, I think she could make it in the CIA. After she finished my interrogation, she went to tell your parents I was here."

Heat crept up Brandi's cheeks. She loved her sister, but there was no telling what the overprotective little half-pint had asked Jake. "It gets worse."

His eyes widened. "What do you mean?"

"I promised Mom and Dad I'd bring you in to meet them. They're in the kitchen."

"Oh. No problem."

Brandi led him to the kitchen and quickly made the introductions. She was thankful her mom kept her dad from continuing Valerie's questioning, and within minutes Brandi and Jake were in his truck zooming off to the party.

The soft country music drifting from the radio took away the pressure to make conversation. Brandi rested her head against the seat. This was her first date in Arkansas. She'd been grief-stricken since her family moved here at the beginning of the school year. Her mom called it pouting. Brandi preferred mourning. But graduation was next week, and then she was California-bound.

"So are you going on the class trip?" Jake's voice jerked her out of her California-dreamin', as her dad called it.

"I don't think so."

"You should. It'll be fun."

"When you've had season tickets to Disneyland, Silver Dollar City doesn't quite cut it."

His smile faltered. "I guess. We're going to Branson, too."

"Country music, my favorite."

At her sarcastic comment the remains of his smile faded, replaced by a wooden expression. He turned the radio off with a snap.

She cringed. Her mom warned her constantly about her sharp tongue. Her brain fumbled for something positive to say. "I. . ." She was at a loss. Sometimes it was best not to say anything.

Out of the abundance of the heart the mouth speaketh. Her dad had slipped that Bible verse from the book of Matthew under her door last week and then given her a lecture that night.

Didn't he see that, if she gave Arkansas a chance in her

heart, it would be a betrayal to all her friends in California? She'd tried to explain it to him often enough, but apparently he couldn't get it.

When they finally arrived at the party, Jake jumped out and opened her door.

"Thanks."

"No problem." His easy manner had vanished; she didn't like the new stiff Jake nearly as well.

"Listen. When I said—"

"Don't worry about it. This isn't California. Never will be. And I'm glad." He raised his chin defiantly. "I thought maybe I'd gotten the wrong impression of you. But I guess I was right in the first place."

Dana's parents opened the door before Brandi could try again to apologize. The couple said hello and disappeared into the huge house. Music reverberated from the sound system. Kids were sitting around in clusters talking as she and Jake wandered into the living room.

"Sodas are in the kitchen—and chips and dip," Dana called from the corner love seat where she was looking through CDs with a couple of juniors.

"You want a soda?" Jake asked.

At least he was talking to her again. "Sure."

They threaded through the crowd to the kitchen. As soon as the door opened, Brandi recognized Tammy Roland and her posse standing by the chips.

૨૦

Jake put a proprietary hand on Brandi's arm. She looked up at him, trying to gauge his expression. Was he protecting her? Or just showing they were together? He guided her toward the drinks without a second glance at Tammy.

Stephanie, one of the girls from Tammy's group, joined Jake and Brandi at the drink table. Just as Brandi took a sip, the girl brushed against her. Brown soda and ice splashed down the front of Brandi's new blue shirt.

"Oh!" Stephanie grabbed napkins and started swiping at the spreading stain. "I'm *so* sorry!"

Jake stood back, obviously unsure what to do with a soda-doused date.

"Here—let me see," Tammy purred, appearing at Brandi's side, sympathy etched on her beautiful face. "Bless your heart. Let's go to the bathroom and get this cleaned up." She smiled at Jake. "I'll have her back to you as good as new in no time."

For a fleeting second Brandi wondered if she'd dreamed every mean thing Tammy had said and done to her since the beginning of the year.

As soon as the two of them were in the bathroom, Tammy grabbed a washcloth and ran warm water over it. "It was really nice of you to go out with Jake." Her voice poured like molasses, slow and sticky.

Tammy pulled the shirt away from Brandi's skin and slopped water onto the front, effectively diluting the soda but drenching the fabric.

"He was so desperate to make me jealous." Tammy tossed her long hair back over her shoulder. "But I guess he told you that."

Brandi stared at her. How could a voice so sweet say such evil things?

"Oh, no." Tammy grimaced and let go of the wet blouse. "He didn't tell you."

The dripping material clung to Brandi's skin. She shivered.

"I'm sorry. Jake is usually nicer than that. I figured since Les told me—"

Brandi snatched the cloth from the brunette's hand. "I think I can handle this."

"In that case I'm going out and give Jake a piece of my

mind for not letting you in on the game." Before Brandi could stop her, Tammy slipped from the room, leaving a cloud of confusion in her wake.

Had Jake really used her? Or was this more of Tammy's lies?

Brandi stayed in the bathroom until her shirt had almost dried. The stain still stood out like a sore thumb, but at least it wasn't soaked.

She walked into the living room and spied Jake, just as Tammy threw her arms around him. Brandi's heart squeezed. She could feel the eyes of her classmates on her.

"Brandi." Jake unlatched Tammy's arms from around his neck and walked over to Brandi. "Are you okay?"

She met Tammy's glittering gaze over his shoulder. "Yes, I'm fine. And so are you, I see." She forced a painful smile. "I'm glad you two worked things out." *You deserve each other.*

Jake blushed. "Do you want us to take you home?"

"No, thanks. I saw Elizabeth in the hall. I'll catch a ride with her."

Brandi held her head high and walked out of the room, praying with every step that God would give her strength to hold back the tears until she was alone.

California, here I come.

one

If Brandi Delaney hadn't known better, she'd have thought she was arriving in Japan in the peak of monsoon season instead of north Arkansas in early autumn. About an hour after she'd crossed the Oklahoma border into the Natural State, the steady downpour that had been her traveling companion escalated into a torrential flood.

Squinting through the windshield, she cranked the wipers to hyperspeed. The *swish-swish, screech-screech* grated on her already taut nerves. Why couldn't her parents have stayed in sunny California where God had finally planted them?

Water gushed down the ditches on either side of the two-lane highway. The potholes in the oft-patched road were filled to the brim, so the last several miles had been like playing dodge ball with nature. She gripped the steering wheel tighter and cast a glance at the convertible top. At least it was waterproof.

Lord, I know I've been asking You for a better attitude about this trip, but now I'm begging You just to get me there safely.

She slowed. Keeping her gaze on the road she felt around in the seat for the little map—exact directions to Delaney's Bed-and-Breakfast. Eight years had passed since she'd lived there with her parents. But before the ink had dried on her high school diploma, she'd escaped back home to California to stay with her grandmother and attend college. She'd never returned.

And in spite of what her family might think, her absence wasn't because she was still angry that they'd ripped her away from her friends, not to mention the beach, right before her senior year. Why would she hold a grudge just because, after finally settling in one place for four years, her parents had uprooted again and moved the Delaney family to the land time forgot?

Okay, maybe she was a little bitter. But she'd kept in touch. The whole family met twice a year in Colorado. That had been enough until a week ago.

That phone call had turned her scheduled life upside-down, and if she was reading the map and her memory right, a low-water bridge and one right turn down a wooded lane were all that stood between her and the chaos her family now called everyday life. She tossed the paper on the passenger seat and peered at the road. The bridge loomed straight ahead.

She stopped the car and stared at the small white slab of concrete. It looked so insignificant. Water gushed across the top, but she'd crossed deeper mud holes in this car so she wasn't worried. Not about the water.

Was she about to cross over to another dimension, another life completely? Give up her hard-won independence and be governed again by her family's needs? She'd driven all the way from California, concentrating on the road trip and avoiding the thought of the end of her journey. But once she drove across that bridge there would be no turning back.

Who was she kidding? There'd been no turning back since she'd discovered Gram needed her.

She inched the compact convertible closer and switched her headlights to bright, stifling an impatient grunt at the delay. She was thankful only a few inches of water rushed across the platform, leaving the solid white concrete still easily visible. Her car was a far cry from the four-wheel-drives that seemed to be native to this area, but it should be able to handle this challenge, as long as she held steady in the center of the one-lane bridge.

She eased the convertible onto the concrete slab then gasped. Could that force be those measly inches of water? With a sudden flash of distant memory she recalled a neighbor cautioning her family about crossing low-water bridges when it was raining. She'd tuned out the dire warning, as she had most everything then, but it had apparently stuck in her subconscious eight years ago, only to surface now a minute too late.

She gripped the steering wheel. No matter how she turned it, though, the car moved at the mercy of the raging current. Brandi's stomach roiled. She fumbled for the switch and rolled down her window. The loud rushing of the water made it hard to think. Should she jump?

Oh, Father. Please help me.

She wiped the rain from her face and peered down at the writhing waves. With a shudder she dropped her head back against the seat, heart slamming against her ribcage, as the car did a slow dance off the bridge into the raging current.

❧

What kind of idiot would drive onto the low-water bridge with the creek rushing across it?

A spoiled California girl with more beauty than brains. Jake McFadden answered his own question as the car turned sideways and swept off into the current. A tiny red convertible. And no doubt the driver was just the person he was looking for.

He'd volunteered to drive out to check on the status of the creek and to be sure Elva's granddaughter, Brandi, hadn't gotten stranded on the other side of the bridge. It had never occurred to them she might be in real danger. But then they'd never imagined her trying to cross with water over the bridge. People who did that most often ended up in cemeteries.

His pulse raced as he threw his truck into park. He jumped out and ducked as rain pelted him like bird shot. Halfway down the creek bank he groaned at his own folly. What power did he have against the raging creek?

He doubled back and grabbed a rope and lanyard from his toolbox. Pain shot through his shoulder. The doctor's words about avoiding a reinjury echoed in his head, but he had no choice. He couldn't let the girl drown. He gritted his teeth against the pain and took off at a dead run down the bank.

The tightness in his chest eased when he saw the red car, upright, wedged in a fork of an old log that protruded into the water. It must be perched on the submerged tree that, judging from the weather-beaten appearance of the huge limbs sticking up out of the water, had lain halfway across the creek for a long time.

He could see Brandi still buckled in the driver's seat. Her window was down, but water hadn't reached the opening yet.

"Don't move!" he yelled, but the words blew back into his face with the driving rain.

He secured the rope to a big oak and tied the other end to his belt. With the lanyard dangling from his belt loop, he heaved himself up onto the fallen tree and inched along the trunk toward the car.

Brandi had unfastened her seat belt and was about to open the door. Every movement rocked the car, threatening to dislodge the vehicle from the safety of its nest in the crook of the tree limbs and send it back into the rapidly flowing water.

"No!" This time she heard him. Even through the downpour he could see her startled blue eyes.

"I have to get out of here! The car isn't stable!" she screamed.

"No kidding," Jake murmured under his breath, carefully weighing each step along the slippery bark. "Be still!" he yelled. "I'll have you out in no time." Just because she'd done something incredibly stu—okay, just because she'd used bad judgment didn't mean she didn't need reassurance.

Where was a good fireman when you needed him? If his

brother Clint were there, he'd know exactly what to do. Instead Brandi was stuck with the youngest McFadden brother—a washed-up pro-baseball player who couldn't hold on to his high school sweetheart, much less rescue a damsel in distress.

He grunted at the unexpected wave of self-loathing. Just last night he'd told his parents he was handling his season-ending shoulder injury fine. They hadn't mentioned Tammy, and neither had he.

His foot slipped, and he sat down hard on the submerged log, catching himself under the water with his right arm. Red-hot pain seared through his shoulder. Nausea washed over him. He bit his tongue to keep from yelling but scrambled to his feet.

He was almost near enough to touch the car when it shifted positions.

Brandi opened the car door.

"Jump!"

Their eyes locked for a moment. She seemed to be considering his command. Jake wondered if she recognized him. His disastrous date with the frosty beauty at the end of their senior year had driven him right back into his ex-girlfriend's arms. And shortly after that, something, although he doubted seriously it had anything to do with him, had propelled Brandi Delaney to California as fast as she could go. Would that fiasco of a date eight years ago cause her to distrust his advice in this crucial moment?

Please, Lord, let her trust me.

"Brandi! Jump now!"

Just as the convertible slipped into the raging current, she leaped into the creek, landing between two large limbs. Jake murmured a prayer of thanks when she quickly grabbed onto the one nearest him.

Her legs and feet were visible just beneath the surface of

the water as the strong force tried to yank her arms from the limb.

"Hold on." Jake tied the rope to a branch as high as he could reach and clipped the loose end of the lanyard onto it.

He straddled the log and, with his legs clasped tight around it, stretched out on his stomach, straining to fasten the lanyard onto her belt loop so she'd be secured by the rope. His shoulder protested, but he pushed harder, trembling with relief when the latch snapped into place.

He forced a calm note of confidence into his voice. "You probably don't remember me, but I'm Jake McFadden. We're going to get you out of here."

"We?" She clutched the branch and looked over his shoulder as if she expected a squadron of Rescue Rangers to be crowded behind him on the log.

"God and me!" he shouted. "Mostly Him."

She barely nodded. "Thanks."

"We'll have you home shortly."

"Okay." Her voice was as weak as the mewling of a newborn kitten.

"Easy—it's going to be fine." He spoke to her in the same tone he used with the horses when they were skittish. Terror glistened in her eyes, but he was thankful for her outward calm. Tammy would have been in hysterics by now. "You can let go of the limb now. I've got you." Ignoring his shoulder pain, he pulled her toward him.

When he held her in his arms, he smoothed back her hair. Even though they were both half-immersed in water, at least it had quit raining. "You'll be home safe and sound in no time, Brandi."

Her eyes, which had been closed, jerked open. "Home?"

He nodded and stared into her unusual blue eyes. He'd forgotten how the brilliant cornflower color was punctuated by white flecks in the shape of a starburst.

She closed her eyes again and relaxed against him, but he could feel her trembling.

"Brandi, pay attention." He felt her tense at his stern tone, but he couldn't afford to be softhearted right now. "I need you to do something for me."

She opened her eyes. "What?"

"I'm going to have to carry you on my back, so I can hold on to the rope with both hands." He looked up at the rope stretched tautly from the branch to the tree on the bank. She was hooked to the rope by the lanyard, but he wasn't. "Wrap your arms around my neck and don't let go."

"Okay."

"Attagirl." Keeping a tight grasp on her, he eased to his feet then reached up and grabbed the rope. After he'd positioned her on his back, he inched along the log. He finally stepped off onto the creek bank and pulled her around in front of him. As soon as he unhooked the lanyard from her belt, he cradled her against his chest and carried her toward the truck. "Delaney's B&B, here we come!" he yelled.

She said something else then, something that sounded almost like a very sarcastic "Yippee."

two

As Jake fumbled the door latch open with his free hand, Brandi desperately wanted to jump down and tell him she could take care of herself. But her legs still felt like a pair of Slinkies. When she was settled in the truck, he grabbed something from beneath the seat, tossed it into her lap then gently closed her door.

Shivering, Brandi gathered the camouflage jacket around her. It smelled like a hunter's closet, but she was grateful for its warmth.

Jake jumped into the driver's side and glanced across at her. "Brandi? How are you feeling?"

She peeked out at him over the collar of the jacket. "Better, thanks."

"With the creek across the bridge it will take about thirty minutes to get to the ER."

"No!" She shook her head. "I'm fine."

He opened his mouth and stared at her, his dark blue eyes wide. Tiny rivulets of water streamed off his hair onto his face.

"Okay, fine might be a stretch, but I don't need a doctor. Please just take me to the B&B." She'd never expected to beg to go there, but right now all she wanted was a warm bath. And a hug from Gram would be nice.

At the beginning of the summer, when Brandi's parents received an offer to join a six-month medical mission trip to Albania, adventurous Gram had jumped at the chance to take an extended trip to Arkansas. For the last month she'd been running the B&B and supervising Brandi's brother and sisters.

The seventy-year-young woman had taken to the new venture like a dolphin to the ocean and had made Brandi feel a part of it with her hour-long weekly phone conversations. Last time she'd called, the older woman had tried to make a joke of her fall down the stairs, but Brandi had known it was serious. When she'd asked if she needed to come to Arkansas, the hesitant silence over the phone line spoke volumes.

So she'd taken a six-month leave of absence from her job as a computer programmer, and here she was. Dripping wet and freezing. She shivered again.

Jake turned on the heat and eased the truck onto the road.

She looked over at the man who had been the cutest guy in her senior class. Some people hit their peak in high school and went gradually downhill from there. That was obviously not the case with him.

"So did you have a nice trip?" As soon as he spoke, she noticed red creep up his cheeks.

She smiled at the silly question. "It was good until the last hour. Then things got a little weird."

"Didn't you notice water was rushing over the bridge?"

She could hear the disbelief in his voice. Funny, that was one big thing she remembered about her senior year. With a seemingly innocuous question the locals could always make her feel so stupid. She bit back the urge to explain and stared at the dashboard.

She wasn't a teenager anymore, and she'd learned a few tactics about dealing with questions that put her on the spot.

After several seconds of silence he cleared his throat. "I guess you didn't know any better."

Actually I knew better, but I almost drowned just to inconvenience you. She bit back the sarcastic retort and glanced over at him. He guided the truck with his left hand, his right arm resting lazily on his leg. Was he trying to accentuate her incompetence by showing how effortlessly he could drive this road?

"What do you do if you're swimming in the ocean and get caught in a riptide?" she asked quietly.

He whipped his gaze around to stare at her then looked quickly back at the road. "I have no idea."

"Strange. I would think anyone would know that."

She regarded his profile. His chiseled lips tilted upward. "Point taken. Sorry." He pulled the truck into the B&B parking lot and ran around to open her door.

"I can walk," she said before he could swoop her into his arms again. Being carried by a strong man was a luxury she had no intention of getting used to. She'd worked too hard to stand on her own two feet.

"You're sure?"

"Yes, thanks." When she stepped from the vehicle, the sun beamed as if in mock celebration of her arrival. Water droplets glistened on the leaves of the lush trees that surrounded the two-story house, giving it a fairy-tale aura.

"Hard to believe it was pouring thirty minutes ago, isn't it?" Jake cupped her elbow with his hand and guided her toward the sidewalk.

Resisting the urge to shake off his helpful grip, she nodded. "But since my car's gone and my clothes are soaking wet, I'm pretty sure it wasn't a dream."

"Want me to pinch you to be positive?" His grin was so unexpectedly mischievous that she giggled.

"Not if you value your life."

"Look at you. I save your life, and you threaten mine."

"Brandi!" Her grandmother's cry from the front door interrupted their bantering. The older woman hobbled down the sidewalk leaning heavily on a cane for support. "What happened?"

"I'm fine, Gram." Brandi ran to meet her. In spite of the dripping clothes Gram quickly folded her into a warm embrace. "It's great to see you," Brandi whispered against her grandmother's shoulder. Tears stung her eyes as she relaxed in the familiar hug and breathed in the honeysuckle scent. How many times in her life had this particular embrace made all her hurts better? Too many to count.

Aware that Jake McFadden stood watching this touching display of sentimentality, Brandi released Gram. The woman's face was pale.

"Where's your car?"

"It washed down the creek."

"That little stream?" Gram grew whiter as she pointed in the direction of the road with a disbelieving look on her face.

Jake cleared his throat. "That 'little stream' is more like a raging river right now." He leveled a gaze at Brandi, and she thought he seemed to be weighing his words. That was a pleasant switch. "Since Brandi isn't familiar with how quickly a creek can rise, she didn't know not to cross. It was a natural mistake."

"I'm thankful Jake was there to save me from the error of my ways." If they were going to play nicey-nice for her grandmother's sake, Brandi wasn't going to be outdone.

❧

Jake took a sip of his coffee and rubbed his aching shoulder with his left hand. After he'd turned Brandi over to her grandmother, he'd called the sheriff to report the loss of her car. Then he'd taken a hot shower and spent the evening with an ice pack. He was glad he had weekends off from both his cardio sessions with Coach and his physical therapy. Maybe his shoulder would be rested by Monday.

Something rustled at the door. He spied the newspaper on the floor and scooped it up. Right down to the morning paper delivery, he loved everything about this place. He sank into the overstuffed chair beside the window to catch up on current events.

Instead of focusing on the words, he kept seeing a drenched waif with big blue eyes. A beautiful blond who made his heart beat faster with every glance. If his problems with Tammy had taught him anything, it was that beauty shouldn't be trusted.

He pulled his attention back to the newsprint; but when he'd read the same sentence three times and still didn't know what it said, he tossed the paper on the table. Things had been going so well at the B&B. Until now.

When the team doctors had sent him home to heal from a shoulder injury and subsequent surgery, he'd decided the smoothly run establishment in his old hometown would be the perfect place to stay. It had a hiking trail behind it for his daily runs. A brisk ten-minute walk through the woods took him to his high school coach's house. They'd been working together twice a day for two months now on cardiovascular strength, and Jake felt more positive about playing ball again than he had since his first surgery.

He couldn't afford the distraction of living in upheaval. His parents had sold the ranch he grew up on to his brother Holt and taken up permanent residence at the lake house. But even with them gone it wasn't as if the B&B were his only option. He could move to a motel or stay with Holt and Megan. They didn't live too far away, and they'd certainly invited him enough times.

He looked at his computer desk, covered with news stories and medical reports. As much as he loved his family, he needed privacy. The Delaneys understood that when he wasn't at Coach Carter's house he was in his room working on his fight against teen drug and alcohol use. Sometimes he made it downstairs for meals. When he didn't, a tray always appeared at his door.

They treated him more like family than a paying guest. And Elva had picked up right where the Delaneys left off. But with Tom and Lynette overseas and Elva hurt, now he was going to be left in the clutches of Miss That's-not-how-we-do-it-in-California, as he'd called her in high school. He massaged his shoulder again. And from the way she'd turned things upside down with her arrival she hadn't changed much in the past eight years.

"Jake?" The whisper drifted into his room from the hallway. Tom and Lynette Delaney didn't allow their kids to knock on guests' doors, but no one had ever mentioned desperate whispers.

He crossed the room and opened the door. Ten-year-old Melissa jerked back from where she'd apparently had her mouth pressed against the crack. Her twelve-year-old brother, Michael, stood behind her, his blond hair sticking out in every direction. A junior inventor, he already had the mad scientist hair down pat.

"M & M! Come in." He stepped back and motioned the inseparable pair into his room. When they didn't grin at his nickname for them, he took a closer look at their troubled faces. "What's up?"

"Brandi's been in bed ever since she got here yesterday afternoon," Michael said.

"Gram is worried about her—I can tell. And Valerie's in her room and won't come out," Melissa added.

Jake smiled sympathetically, thinking about the pouting seventeen-year-old. "She's still mad."

Michael frowned. "Do you think Brandi's gonna be as

mean as Valerie says she will?"

Both sets of blue eyes looked up at him, begging for reassurance. He took a deep breath and pushed his earlier thoughts aside. "I'm sure Brandi wouldn't mistreat you guys. Valerie's just upset."

"Who's not?" Melissa snorted. "Mom and Dad should just come home."

"Yeah, right. Like that's gonna happen. Maybe my time machine will start working, too," Michael said. "I told you, you're making a big deal out of nothing." He looked at Jake. "Isn't she?"

Before Jake could speak, Melissa jumped in, her blond braids practically quivering with indignation. "Nothing? Even if she is our sister, we only see Brandi twice a year. Maybe we don't really know her at all. What if she locks us in our rooms and gives us nothing but bread and water?"

Michael shook his head. "You read too much."

Melissa muttered something about his not being able to survive without homemade pizza.

Jake bit back a laugh. "Why don't you two go check on breakfast, and let's just see how things go?"

"Wait." Melissa grabbed his arm. "We need you to promise us something."

"What?" Jake asked. With these two there was no telling.

"Promise you won't leave."

"You know I plan to be here until right before Christmas."

The children looked at each other. "That's when Mom and Dad are coming back."

Relief flooded their tan faces, and they hurried from the room. As the door closed behind them, Jake felt a flash of irritation at Valerie. She'd allowed her jealousy to scare her younger brother and sister. Though she'd never see it, this kind of thing was the reason her parents and then her grandmother hadn't left her in charge.

But whether they'd made the right choice by putting Miss California Beauty Queen in command of the B&B remained to be seen.

three

Brandi rolled over and snuggled under the covers as warmth streamed across her face. Even with her eyes shut she could see light. She eased one eye open. Sunshine? Why hadn't her alarm gone off? Her heart pounded. She hated being late. She sat up quickly, and for a minute the unfamiliar room seemed to tilt on its axis.

She shook her head to clear away the confusion. The motion seemed to jar loose a flood of memories that gushed into her mind with the force of an out-of-control creek. Had her car really washed off a bridge? Or had it been a dream? At least until she recognized him, the handsome rain-drenched hero would have been dream material; but the rest would have to be classified as a nightmare.

She pulled the covers up to her shoulders and ran her finger absently over the bright red-and-yellow square pattern. The colorful quilt faded from her vision as scenes played in her mind. Her car tumbling into the raging creek. A partially submerged log catching the little convertible. And finally Jake McFadden urging her to jump into the water.

She shuddered. It was no dream. Her terror had been real. She'd thought she was going to die. But Jake had rescued her. And if that part was real, then she must be at the Delaney B&B.

Alive and well and still bound to keep her promise to her grandmother.

She flopped back down on the bed and pulled the blankets over her head. She needed time to sort this out.

Eyes closed against the soft velour blanket, she breathed in the fabric softener scent and remembered soaking in a warm bath and slipping into a clean gown Gram had provided. Then she'd collapsed into the bed. How long ago had that been?

A tap sounded on the door, and Brandi quickly yanked the covers off her head. "Yes?"

The wooden door squeaked open. Gram stood in the archway leaning on her cane, holding a steaming coffee cup in her other hand. "Good morning, honey."

"Hi, Gram."

Her grandmother slowly closed the distance between them, set the cup on the nightstand, and wrapped her in a hug.

Tears stung Brandi's eyes as she realized the woman had negotiated the stairs with a cup of coffee for her beloved granddaughter. "Thanks for the coffee. I've missed you." She pushed back and looked at the older woman. "Did you say morning?" Had she been in bed since yesterday afternoon?

"Yes." She squeezed Brandi's hand. "I know I saw you then, but it's so good to see you—"

"Dry?" Brandi took a sip of her coffee.

"No. Well, yes, but I was going to say awake and looking none the worse for the wear." She smiled and ran her hand over Brandi's hair. "I'm just thanking God Jake showed up in time to save you."

"Yeah, Jake McFadden—a real hometown hero." She almost cringed at the sarcasm in her voice. He may have been a jerk in high school, but the man had just saved her life. She cleared her throat. "I'm very glad he was there."

Gram arched a brow and nodded.

"I can't wait to see the kids. I can't believe I fell asleep before they got home from school yesterday and never woke up. I'm surprised Valerie hasn't already been in here." Brandi grinned. Valerie, nine years her junior, had hero-worshipped

Brandi since before she'd left for California. Her sister's unconditional acceptance had been a balm for Brandi's smarting conscience at leaving her family.

An odd look crossed her grandmother's face, quickly followed by a smile that didn't quite match the worry in her eyes. "I promised everyone I'd see if you were up to coming down for breakfast."

"Up to it? Do I smell pancakes?"

"Chocolate chip. You remember Nellie, don't you?"

Brandi smiled. Nellie had started working for the Delaneys' right after they moved here. Her cooking had been the only thing from Brandi's year in Arkansas that she hadn't wanted to forget. "Of course." She could almost taste the pancakes. "Yum." She held up her empty cup. "Any more of this chocolate-velvet coffee down there?"

"A whole pot."

"What am I supposed to wear?"

"I brought in some outfits from your mom's closet I thought might work for you until you can get to the store. They're hanging in the armoire. I also put a new toothbrush and a few other necessities in the bathroom. Of course, there's still a chance your stuff will be recovered. . . ."

Brandi thought of her last glimpse of the red car tumbling along with the water. She shook her head. "Somehow I doubt it."

"I'm so sorry, honey." Gram reached out and caressed her cheek.

Brandi cupped her grandmother's hand in her own and squeezed it. "It's nothing that can't be replaced. Thanks for the clothes. Give me half an hour to shower and dress, and I'll be there with bells on."

Gram kissed her forehead. "It'll take this old woman that long to get back downstairs."

"You are not old!" Brandi protested.

"Let's just say I'm thrilled you're here and leave it at that." She grinned. "And I'm glad I stayed in your parents' room downstairs so I could be close to Michael and Melissa. I think this will be my last trip up those stairs for a while."

"I'll take care of everything." Brandi couldn't quite smile, faced with the evidence of her grandmother's frailty.

"You're going to do great. I appreciate your coming. Now get dressed, and I'll race you downstairs." Gram grinned and slipped out the door.

When she was alone again, Brandi stood and stretched. Her arms were sore from holding on to the tree limb in the water. She wondered if Jake felt any ill effects from her bad judgment. She should probably find out where he lived so she could call him and thank him properly.

She found a Bible in the top drawer of the nightstand. That hadn't changed. Her parents always made sure there was one in every room. This morning she needed the constancy of her daily devotional, even if it had to be an abbreviated version.

After she finished reading a passage in Philippians and thanking God again for keeping her safe, she quickly showered and dressed. As she applied a touch of lipstick from the tube Gram had left her, she thought about her dark-haired rescuer. He was a mystery to her. And she'd always fancied herself a mystery-solver.

In high school she'd been attracted to him, in spite of the fact he was part of the crowd that made her life miserable. When he asked her out, she saw a side of him she thought she would like to know better. Instead he'd allowed Tammy to reel him neatly back in, without so much as a backward glance for Brandi. She'd known then, without a doubt, that he wouldn't walk across the road to help her out of a ditch.

But yesterday, apparently without hesitation, he'd risked

his life to save hers.

And since the moment she'd decided to trust him and jump into the swirling water, she couldn't get him out of her mind. Had he changed that much? Or had she been wrong about him back then?

She snatched a pair of sandals from the closet and slipped into them. She was safer concentrating on her hunger pains and leaving the mystery of Jake McFadden to someone else. She slipped into the hall and looked in the open doors as she walked by.

Even after all these years her parents had kept her idea of naming each room after a famous classic movie. She smiled as she passed IT'S A WONDERFUL LIFE and THE WIZARD OF OZ. They had allowed her to do it because they desperately wanted her to be happy in Arkansas, and she'd gone ahead with the project because naming and decorating the rooms accordingly had made life bearable for a while.

She'd figured her mom would redo them at the first opportunity. But to her surprise over the years her family had occasionally told funny stories about guests, like the eccentric woman who'd stayed in GONE WITH THE WIND or the family in STAGECOACH who had done something odd.

Gram walked into the foyer as Brandi reached the bottom step. "Who's going to ring the bell for breakfast?" she called.

"I am!" Melissa ran into the room then skittered to a stop when she saw Brandi.

Was that fear in her little sister's eyes? Admittedly she'd been two years old when Brandi moved back to California, but they'd remained close. Or at least Brandi thought they had. Maybe Melissa was just going through a shy stage.

"Hey, Melissa." Brandi held out her arms. The little girl gave her a stiff hug then quickly retreated. "Where's Michael?" Brandi asked, hoping to entice her out of her shell a bit. What had happened to the bright, curious girl she remembered?

"Waiting in the dining room." Melissa grabbed the brass bell from the small marble-top table and looked at her grandmother. "Ready, Gram?"

"Sure, hon."

Melissa stood straight, shoulders back, and held the bell aloft with great ceremony. At her grandmother's nod she swung the brass bell back and forth, flinching as the loud noise filled the house.

When the tone faded away, Brandi grinned. "Good job, sis."

"Thanks." Melissa set the bell back in its place and ran to the dining room.

"Still the drama queen, I see," Brandi whispered.

Gram frowned and looked up the empty stairs. "Unfortunately she's not the only one around here."

"What do you mean?" Gram had the same expression she'd had earlier when Brandi had mentioned Valerie. Her teenage sister still hadn't appeared. Was that who Gram was talking about?

Gram glanced back at Brandi as if she'd forgotten she was there then shook her head. "Let's go eat. We can talk later."

Michael looked up when she came in. To her relief he returned her wink and clambered to his feet to give her a one-arm speed hug. She smoothed his hair down and smiled as it stuck straight out again. He ducked from her hand, grinning. As he got closer to official teenagerhood, his reluctance to show affection warred with his naturally affectionate personality.

Unlike Melissa's sudden standoffishness and Valerie's failure to appear, Brandi didn't take Michael's growing pains personally. And the unspoken rule of the house was that after the bell rang everyone had five minutes to come to the table, so maybe Valerie would still show up.

Brandi sank into the chair between her brother and her

grandmother and admired the sumptuous spread of food. The delicious aroma wafted up her nose and straight into the hungry corners of her soul. She might have to snitch a pancake to tide her over.

The oval oak table was set for six. She, Michael, Melissa, and Gram were anxiously waiting, so that left two still to come.

When Gram hurt her back, she'd had to cancel the next few weeks of reservations. Now that Brandi was here, she had two weeks to get used to things before business resumed as normal. But there was one permanent guest in CASABLANCA. Gram hadn't told her much about him on the phone, but Brandi did know he ate meals with the family, rather than in the guest dining room.

As they chatted about the food, Gram cast an irritated glance at one of the empty seats—presumably the one Valerie usually occupied. Brandi looked at her watch. Five minutes were up. If Valerie and their permanent guest were coming, they'd better hurry.

Movement in the doorway brought her gaze up to meet the eyes of her rescuer. Jake McFadden had come to breakfast.

"I'm sorry I'm late."

"That's fine," Gram murmured, as Jake slipped easily into one of the empty chairs.

Realization hit Brandi like a lightning bolt. Hometown hero Jake McFadden lived at the Delaney B&B. And she was about to become his gracious hostess. Sometimes she felt like laughing at life's little ironies. Unfortunately this wasn't one of those times.

❧

"Jake? Will you offer thanks for the food?" Elva asked softly.

Jake nodded. During his years on the road, both with baseball and his speaking program, he hadn't found a lot of time for prayer. But since his injury he spent as much or more time talking to God as he did to anyone.

He bowed his head and concentrated on clearing his mind of distractions, especially the blue-eyed one across the table who was peering at him as if he were pond scum. "Father, thank You for this wonderful time of homecoming and reunion. Thank You for providing this food for us. Please continue to bless this house with peace and prosperity. Watch over us always. In Jesus' name, amen."

He looked up, and this time he didn't try to avoid Brandi's gaze. His family was big on second chances. Maybe she deserved one.

Maybe he did, too.

"So, Brandi"—he helped himself to a couple of pancakes— "can you cook as well as your mom and your grandmother?"

She narrowed her eyes. "Probably not, but I'm pretty sure I can keep you guys from starving on Nellie's days off."

Oh, great. He'd managed to insult her without even trying. "No doubt."

"Brandi always loved to cook." Elva looked fondly at her oldest granddaughter. "I remember when you used to come in from the beach and throw my big apron over your bathing suit. We got a kick out of that. You, with your flip-flops and neon-colored suit, wearing a chef's apron that hung down to your ankles."

"Don't we have a picture of that somewhere?" Michael asked.

Jake watched with fascination as Brandi's face turned a becoming shade of pink.

"Please. No pictures," she pleaded.

"What about autographs?" Jake quipped.

She leveled him with a gaze that left little doubt concerning how she felt about sharing her intimate childhood memories with him. "I'll leave the autographs to you, superstar."

Elva choked on the orange juice she was sipping. Jake saw pain flash across her face with each cough.

Brandi patted her grandmother gently on the back, but she kept a razor-sharp gaze on Jake. He could see the unexplained animosity she'd always had for him rippling beneath the surface of those beautiful blue eyes.

He rubbed his aching shoulder. So much for second chances. She hadn't changed a bit.

four

As soon as she knew Gram was okay, Brandi pushed to her feet, leaving her pancakes half eaten. Her appetite had fled along with her good sense as soon as Jake McFadden walked into the room. "If you'll excuse me, I need to check on some things upstairs."

She ignored her grandmother's startled expression and strode from the room, head held high. When she was safely in the foyer she ran, taking the stairs two at a time. She hesitated for a second outside Valerie's room, struggling to get a handle on her temper.

Life spun around her in a dizzying whirl, and she needed to be in control of something right now. Valerie was as good a place to start as any. She tapped on the door. "Val?" She hoped the childhood nickname would soften her sister's heart and get her to open up about what was keeping her in her room.

"Go away."

Brandi arched an eyebrow at the oak-stained door. "I don't think so." She twisted the knob. Locked. "Valerie, let me in. Now."

"Who died and left you boss?"

"I need to talk to you." Brandi kept her voice even. She'd provided enough entertainment for the breakfast crowd without their overhearing this confrontation. "I have something important to ask you."

She heard rustling in the room. Had her appeal to Valerie's innate curiosity worked?

The doorknob rattled.

Brandi tried it again, and it turned easily under her hand. When she stepped into the room, her heart ached. Valerie sat on the window seat, with her back to Brandi. Her arms were wrapped around her knees in a classic defensive posture, and discarded tissues littered the seat and the floor around her. Her thick hair formed a curtain so Brandi couldn't see her face.

"Val? What's wrong?"

Valerie's shoulders raised and dropped, and Brandi hurried over to wrap her in a hug. The girl remained rigid at first; then she collapsed, sobbing, into Brandi's embrace. "Everything."

Brandi sat down on the seat and smoothed back her sister's wild mane of hair. "Start at the beginning."

Valerie pulled away and met her gaze with red puffy eyes. Her whole face was swollen from crying. "When Mom and Dad decided to go to Albania, I asked them to let me run the B&B. I only have half days in school this year anyway. As close as I am to graduating, I could have gotten my GED and been fine. All my friends who are homeschooled do that."

Brandi nodded, not because she agreed, but to let Valerie know she was listening.

"But they asked Gram, which I was fine with. It's been fun to spend some time with her."

"Yeah, she's pretty cool, isn't she?"

Valerie nodded. "I thought so. Then when she got hurt I thought sure she'd let me manage things until Mom and Dad got back." She turned and looked out the window.

After a minute of silence passed, Brandi spoke. "But she and Mom and Dad decided to call me. And now you feel like they didn't think you were capable of handling things."

Valerie rubbed her nose with her hand. "Right."

Brandi handed her a clean tissue from the box on the windowsill. "Valerie, I'm sure they know you're capable."

Valerie snorted. "Right," she said again. This time sarcasm dripped from the word.

"School is important."

"Yeah, yeah." Valerie stood and walked to the bed where she flounced down hard enough to pop a spring. "I've heard it all before. So what did you want to ask me?"

"May I borrow some clothes?"

A hint of a grin flitted across Valerie's face as she gave Brandi a once-over. "You mean color-coordinated pantsuits aren't your new style?"

Brandi grimaced and glanced down at the neat-looking pantsuit. "Mom always looks great, and I'm thankful for the loan, even if it was through Gram; but I'm already having an identity crisis, and these clothes aren't helping." She took in Valerie's frayed bell-bottom jeans and torn top. When had her fashion-conscious sister started dressing like a hippie throwback? "I need something neat enough to go into town."

"Say no more." Valerie opened a drawer and pulled out one pair of khaki pants and a pair of denim capris. The next drawer yielded two tops, and she passed the bundle of clothing to Brandi.

"Thanks. What about a dress for church tomorrow?"

Valerie crossed to the closet and pulled out a simple blue dress. "Will this do?"

"Perfect." Brandi threw the dress across her arm and clasped the other clothes to her chest. "Thanks, sis. I owe you one."

"I'll remind you of that sometime."

Brandi considered her sister's still-somber face. She wanted to ask about Jake McFadden. But in spite of the shared confidences she didn't think she'd gotten to the bottom of Valerie's problem yet, so Jake would have to wait. "What else is bothering you?"

The teen shrugged again. "Just stuff. Things I have to figure out on my own."

Brandi nodded. That hurt, but it was understandable. Even though Valerie had hero-worshipped her, she didn't know her very well anymore. "I'll be praying it all works out."

Valerie mumbled something that could have as easily been "Don't bother" as "Thanks."

"I'd better get busy, Val—Valerie." Michael hadn't been able to say Valerie when he was little, so he'd settled on Val. The rest of the family had followed suit, and it was a habit Brandi had never dropped. But for all Brandi knew, Valerie hated the nickname. "I'm counting on you to work with me. I can't do it without you."

Valerie rolled her eyes. "Did you learn that psychology junk in college?"

Brandi bit back the urge to assure her sister it was true, that she did need her. Instead she nodded. "Yeah. It was in an obscure class called 'How to Deal with Stubborn Teenage Sisters.' You'll be glad to know I made an A."

"Sounds like a class I had—'How to Live with a Stranger Who Suddenly Takes Over Your Home.' Unfortunately I flunked."

Ouch.

Valerie put on her headphones and turned away.

Brandi considered her sister's back for a minute then slipped quietly from the room clutching her borrowed clothes. In spite of the earlier breakthrough the score was definitely Valerie—one, Brandi—zero.

๏

With every thud of his feet on the packed dirt of the hiking trail, Jake imagined firing the ball into the catcher's mitt. "Stri–i–ike three!" the ump screamed to the imaginary batter.

Keep pushing, Jake. You have to stay in shape if you're ever going to pitch again. He didn't mind running, especially today. He was glad to sweat off some of the tension left over from breakfast. If the fire in her eyes at the table was any indication, whatever gratitude Brandi Delaney felt for his saving her life had worn off once she was dry.

Eight years ago, when Brandi had been so sarcastic about their senior trip plans on the way to Dana's party, he'd suspected she regretted going out with him. Tammy had confirmed his suspicions. He'd done Brandi a favor and let her off the hook. Yet, after all these years, she still glared at him and went after him with her sharp tongue every chance she got. It made no sense.

He grimaced at the burning in his lungs as he came out of the trail right behind the B&B. He'd pushed himself too hard while he was thinking about Brandi. When would he learn not to try to understand women? Especially beautiful women?

Maybe she was unhappy with her most recent manicure and was taking it out on him. But if running until he couldn't breathe didn't get her off his mind, what would?

"Jake, heads up!"

A football bobbled through the air and fell at his feet.

Michael Delaney ran forward to pick it up. "Sorry. I can't get the hang of throwing this."

Jake nodded to show he couldn't quite talk yet and leaned forward, hands on his knees. "No problem."

"I've been thinking about going out for football."

"You have?" Jake struggled to keep the surprise from his voice. Ever since Jake had known him, the boy with the slight build had been busy either on the computer or working on a new invention.

"Yeah. Melissa thinks it's a stupid idea, but I'll get better if I practice, right?"

"Sure." Jake wiped his face on his sleeve. "Let me show you how to hold the ball, okay?"

For the next fifteen minutes he worked with Michael, but at the end of the time the boy shook his head. "Melissa's right. I'm never going to get the hang of it."

"If you want to badly enough, you can," Jake said. "I've got to go get a shower right now before lunch, but we can work together some more later."

"Really?" A grin covered Michael's face. "That would be super."

Jake left the boy tossing the ball a foot in the air and then catching it. Or dropping it, whichever the case happened to be.

When Jake walked into the B&B, Brandi was coming down the stairs.

She dropped her gaze to his damp T-shirt then hurried into the den, apparently afraid she'd get dirty by association.

"Hmph," Jake muttered under his breath. "I guess men don't sweat in California."

❧

"Brandi?" Melissa stood in the open doorway of the den, eyes wide.

"Yeah, squirt. What's up?" Brandi grinned at her youngest sister. It seemed like just yesterday she was a chubby-cheeked baby with straight fine blond hair. Now her hair hung in two neat braids down her back, and her delicate features were losing their babyish qualities. If the years from ten to eighteen went as fast as the years from two to ten had, Brandi knew Melissa would be graduating from high school in the blink of an eye. Or sixteen blinks, since Brandi only saw her twice a year. The thought sent a stab of pain through her heart.

"Are you mad because you had to come home and take care of us?"

Brandi cringed at the word "home." She loved her family, but this would never be home. Home was childhood memories of Gram's house, sandy beaches, close friends. "Mad? Of course not."

"Really?"

Brandi walked over and pulled Melissa into a one-armed embrace. "Melissa, why would you think that? I'm happy to be with you all."

Melissa leaned against her sister. "Valerie said you were gonna be mad. And at breakfast you glared really hard and left pancakes on your plate."

That had been the clincher, Brandi realized. Leaving Nellie's chocolate chip pancakes was unheard of, so naturally Melissa knew something was wrong.

Brandi plopped into the rocker and pulled Melissa onto her lap. The little girl snuggled against her. Brandi's heart swelled with emotion. *How must it feel to be ten and have your mother a world away?* She remembered how hard it had been for her when she was eighteen, knowing her mom wouldn't be in to say good night. Of course she'd had Gram. And it had been her choice.

She realized Melissa was still waiting for an explanation. Playing with one of her sister's braids, she lowered her voice. "To tell you the truth, I was a little bit put out at Jake."

"Why?"

Brandi pursed her lips. How could she explain the intricacies of adolescent social situations to a ten-year-old? "Something he did a long time ago hurt my feelings."

"Mama always says we should 'forgive and forget.' Can't you do that with Jake?"

"Sure, baby," Brandi said and squeezed her sister's hand. "I will." She thought she already had, but that seemed to be easier said than done.

⋰⋱

"Explain to me again why you and I are doing laundry and Michael and Melissa are out playing *football*."

Brandi grinned. "C'mon, Val. Don't tell me they never work when you're goofing off."

"If you say so." Valerie rolled her eyes.

Valerie still had a major attitude, but at least she had rejoined the land of the living after Brandi's talk with her. She'd even graced them with her presence at lunch.

"Would you run up and sort these towels into the bathrooms?" Brandi motioned to the color-coded stacks of neatly folded towels. Each bathroom had a different color for its accessories.

"Okay." The teen picked up a pile and balanced it on one arm while getting another one. "The way Jake was looking at you at lunch, I'd think you'd want an excuse to walk by his room later. You might run into him in the hall." Valerie ducked and darted up the stairs.

Brandi smiled and shook her head. Valerie had quite an imagination. Either that or she just thought Jake was cute and decided to make up something. Probably the latter.

Brandi and Jake hadn't even spoken at lunch, but from his and Gram's conversation, she gathered Jake was in town working on his cardio fitness while he waited for his shoulder to heal. He'd be rejoining the Cardinals as soon as he was completely well.

As far as Brandi was concerned, the sooner the better. His blue eyes mesmerized her, but there was no way she'd give a second thought to a man who traveled for a living.

five

"What's the matter with you? You're running like a girl today." The old coach frowned.

Jake pulled off his cap and wiped the sweat from his face. "I guess I'm protecting my shoulder. I strained it a little Friday."

"How?"

Jake thought of the red car being tossed into the creek like a toy sailboat. Explaining sounded too much like tooting his own horn. "Just doing something for Elva." After all, she *had* been the one who'd asked him to go check on Brandi.

Coach Carter shook his head. "Elva Reynolds is a fine woman, Jake. Not to mention a fine-looking one. And I can understand you wantin' to help her." The coach bent down and nimbly scooped a baseball from the grass. "But you pay to stay there. And if you want to be back on the pitcher's mound, you're going to have to be more careful about what you do." He grinned, mischief glinting in his eye. "Next time she needs some heavy lifting done, have her call me."

"Will do, Coach." He suddenly remembered the older couple sitting together at the last church potluck. And even though Jake had sat on the opposite side from Brandi and her family during worship yesterday, after it was over he'd overheard Coach in the foyer asking Brandi about her grandmother.

Attraction was a funny thing. He couldn't imagine a more unlikely pair than the crusty old coach and the vibrant, youthful grandmother. Unless it was he and Brandi.

He frowned. That *would* be unlikely. Impossible was more like it.

"Don't worry about it. You're getting stronger every day." Apparently misreading Jake's frown, Coach patted him on his good shoulder. "In no time you'll be back on top."

"Thanks."

"But for today we might as well call it quits. Give your shoulder a break, and I'll see you back out here tomorrow."

"Yes, sir."

They shook hands, and Jake walked to his truck. As he reached for the door handle, his cell phone rang.

"Hello."

"Jake. Sheriff Baines here. I thought you might want to know we located that little red car you called me about. It caught on a snag a quarter of a mile below the bridge."

"Is it still there?"

"Sure is. On dry land now since the creek's gone down. You'll need to go through the Slaytons' field road to get to it, but they won't mind."

"Thanks, sheriff."

Jake disconnected and called his friend Les.

"Tow service."

"Les, it's Jake. Any chance you can meet me down below the Big Creek bridge with a tow truck in a few minutes?"

"You betcha," he said without hesitation.

"Thanks, Les. I appreciate it."

"For the man who got me season tickets? Anytime."

Jake winced. He'd hoped Les would do it for his high school friend, not his ticket to the major league games. But right now he'd take what he could get. "See you there shortly."

Ten minutes later the two men stood by the car. The back end of the convertible now balanced up in the air on a dead-wood snag, and the front rested on the sandy dirt.

Jake looked inside. "It looks like the things in the backseat didn't get wet."

"Yeah, Miss California ought to be real happy to get that laptop back intact."

When they were in school Jake had called Brandi Miss That's-not-how-we-do-it-in-California, but Les, like a typical teenage boy, had focused on her beauty and quickly shortened it to Miss California. Even though Jake thought of her that way sometimes, too, hearing Les say it had always grated on his nerves.

"Anyone would be glad to get their things back."

"You're as testy about that girl as you ever were, aren't you? No wonder Tammy was so jealous of her." He finished hooking things up and slapped his hands together.

"Tammy wasn't jealous of Brandi." Jake shook his head. Where did Les get such crazy ideas?

"Was so. When you weren't around, her claws came out every time Brandi's name was so much as mentioned. Meow!"

Jake groaned inwardly. Les had been easier to take in high school.

"Hey, I know how you can make some points with Miss California."

"Les, I'm not interested in making points with *Brandi*." He emphasized her name. "I'm just trying to help her because she has a lot to deal with right now."

"Uh huh. I see. Well, then, if you want to *help* her"—Les waggled his eyebrow—"you should call Quinton down at the shop and see if he can get this baby road-ready in the next day or so."

"What about her insurance?"

"Quinton will help her figure all that out when it's done. It's not like it would hurt you if you had to kick in some money at the end. So as long as it doesn't cost her, how could she complain?"

Jake couldn't believe how tempting the idea was. Brandi

had so much going on, recovering from her dip in the creek and trying to take over for Elva. Wouldn't she be thrilled to see her convertible drive into the B&B parking lot?

"C'mon, Jake." Les clamped Jake's sore shoulder with a meaty paw. "Surprise her."

≈

Brandi stretched across the bed and tucked in the sheet. This was the last guest room to be cleaned. And only a little over a week before the first guests arrived. She made a face. Maybe her friends were right. She probably did overprepare to some extent.

She had to admit she'd been a tiny bit disappointed that Jake's room wasn't on the cleaning schedule. She certainly hadn't planned on snooping, but she couldn't help but be curious about a baseball player who spent so many hours locked in his room.

In the six days since she'd arrived, she'd seen almost nothing of him. Not that she was complaining. According to Gram, he picked up clean sheets and towels each week from the linen closet and handled his room chores himself. Did that mean he had something to hide?

She rolled her eyes at her overactive imagination. He probably spent his time stretched out on the couch, watching TV and munching on chips. She removed the chips from her mental picture and replaced them with raw carrots and broccoli. Jake was way too buff to be a junk-food junkie.

"Brandi?" Michael stuck his head in the doorway. "Telephone."

"Thanks. Want to put the bedspread on for me?"

"Sure. Just what I always wanted to do after school. Make beds." His grin belied the words. "I think that's what I'll invent next. An automatic bed-maker."

"Let me know when you finish it. I'll be your first customer."

Brandi left her brother muttering about patents and licenses and ran to grab the extension in her room. "Hello?"

"Bran! It's me."

"Kris, how're you doing?"

"Dying of loneliness since you left."

Brandi grinned. Krista Huntington didn't know the first thing about loneliness. Even though she and Brandi had been best friends since eighth grade, bubbly Krista had enough friends to start her own sit-com.

"Yeah, right."

"I have! After all, I don't lead the exciting life you do. I can't remember the last time my car washed off a bridge and I was rescued by a pro-ball player."

"Be quiet." Brandi laughed. "Gram said you called while I was asleep that first night. I see she filled you in. I tried to call you back, but I got your machine."

"Still prejudiced against answering machines, huh?"

"I like voices to have a real person connected to them. What's wrong with that?" Brandi stretched out on her stomach on the bed. "Besides, I knew you'd call back when you saw my number on caller ID. And I was right."

"Smarty, for your information I didn't even see that you'd phoned."

"Ah, so what's wrong?"

"Wrong?"

"Yep, something must be, or you wouldn't have broken the sacred chain of phone call order to call me back a second time without knowing I called you."

"You make me dizzy even long distance. All those 'calls' and I don't have a clue what you said." For someone who knew Krista as well as Brandi did, her tone screamed evasiveness.

"But something *is* wrong." Silence hummed through the line. Brandi traced the smooth surface of the curly cord with her fingers. Her stomach clenched.

Déjà vu.

She was seventeen again, stranded in Arkansas. Krista was calling from the coast, telling her that Colby—I'll-never-forget-you-no-matter-how-far-away-you-are Colby—had started going out with the homecoming queen. In the wake of that news Brandi had toppled into that infamous date with Jake.

"Not exactly wrong." Krista spoke slowly, as if that would make the news, whatever it was, easier to take. "It's Mitch. He and Norma drove to Vegas and got married." She spit out the last sentence in sharp contrast to her earlier slow speech. It was as if she couldn't stand the words in her mouth another second.

Still clutching the phone, Brandi rolled over onto her back. She stared up at the fan whirring on the plaster ceiling.

"Brandi? Say something."

My life is a ceiling fan, and I'm only a speck of dust holding on for dear life. Hysteria bubbled in her throat. Krista would think she'd lost her mind if she started waxing poetic. "What is there to say? I broke it off with him. You know that."

"Yeah, but I thought someday he'd see you were right and he was too controlling. . . ." Krista's voice drifted off.

"Instead he found someone malleable and ran off to Vegas. I'm okay with that. Really." As she spoke the words she realized they were true. She'd broken things off with Mitch because he wanted to micromanage every detail of her life, but in truth she hadn't loved him as she should. If she had, her heart would be broken right now instead of just a little bruised. Or was that her ego smarting because he'd replaced her so quickly and so permanently?

"You sure?"

"Positive."

"He was a jerk, and you're lucky to be rid of him."

"Aw, c'mon, Kris. Don't sugarcoat your true feelings on my account."

When their laughter died away, Krista cleared her throat. "I miss you, Bran."

"You, too."

She and Krista caught up on all the happenings both at the beach and at the B&B. Twenty minutes later Brandi hung up the phone with a sigh and rolled over onto her back again. So Mitch was married. When she'd broken it off, he'd vowed to change and win her back, but apparently she hadn't been worth the effort. Not with Norma waiting in the wings ready to step into the role of adoring wife. Even though Brandi was thankful to be out of the relationship, that thought still stung.

At least she was still thinking for herself and standing on her own two feet. A little too literally, since she didn't have a vehicle. Without her car she felt so dependent. And that made getting it back or replacing it her top priority.

❧

Jake stared at the Jake McFadden/Stop Drug and Alcohol Use among Teens Web site statistics. Had the number of visitors to the site really fallen off that much since he'd been hurt? He'd have to contact his Webmaster and see if he could link to more sites.

He closed the graph page and reclined slightly in his seat. As he sorted through PR ideas, someone pounded on the door. He leaped to his feet, and his chair rolled back. No one ever even tapped on his door. The house must be on fire.

He crossed the room in three strides and yanked the door open.

Brandi Delaney stood in the hall, fist raised to pound again. Had she lost her mind? She had a bandanna around her hair and a duster tucked in the front pocket of her jeans, but she looked more like a furious queen than a mad maid. If she'd said, "Off with your head!" Jake wouldn't have been surprised.

Her voice, when it came, was chillingly calm, in stark contrast to the violence of her knock. "What have you done with my car?"

Jake gulped. Why did he suddenly feel like a common criminal?

She stepped into the room and looked around. "Where's my car?"

What? Did she think he'd hidden it under the bed?

This wasn't how he'd imagined it at all. After working extra long hours Quinton had promised to have the little red convertible ready by this afternoon. Jake had planned to coax Brandi into going to town with him and then surprise her.

"Surprise?" He flashed her a weak grin.

"Please explain." Her starburst eyes glittered like fireworks.

"The sheriff called a couple of days ago—"

"Three days."

"What?"

"He said he called you *three* days ago."

Jake nodded. "Okay, three days. Anyway, he called while I was out at Coach's and said they'd found your car, about a quarter of a mile down the creek. On dry land."

"And so, of course, since it was *my* car you called me immediately." She tapped her finger on her cheek and glared at him.

Jake took a deep breath and counted to ten silently. Brandi must have written the old adage "Nice guys finish last." Either that or she saw it as her life-long duty to make it come true. So much for trying to do her a favor. "I called my friend Les. Remember him?" From Brandi's snort he guessed she did indeed remember Les. "He owns a tow service. I was going to have him haul it over here and surprise you."

She walked across the room and looked out his bedroom window then turned back to face him. "Where did he park it?"

"I reconsidered and had him take it to Quinton's shop. He's the best around, and I knew he'd do it fast and reasonably priced."

"I don't believe it! Did you call my insurance company and tell them it had been found?" She paced as she talked.

Jake felt the heat creep up his ears and spread to his cheeks. That had been the only part of the whole scheme he was uncomfortable with. "Since you'd already essentially filed a claim, Quinton was able to deal with them. If you have any balance, I'll be glad to pay it."

"Mighty big of you to be willing to bail me out like that." She stopped pacing and faced him, hands on her hips.

"Look—I was trying to be nice. I don't appreciate your attitude."

"No. *You* look. *Your* attitude is the problem. Just because I'm a blond whose features are put together in an okay way, you think I don't have sense enough to handle my own business. So, being the big strong he-man you are—"

"I'm sorry." He interrupted her, partly to stop her from saying anything else, but he meant the apology. She had no idea how sorry he was that he'd gotten involved. Why he'd ever tried to do something for her, he didn't know. "I should have called you. You just had so much going on that I thought I could help."

His apology seemed to roll right off her righteous anger.

She pushed to her feet. "This discussion is a waste of time. Is Quinton going to be able to fix the car?"

"He should have it done this afternoon. As good as new."

"Great." She grabbed the doorknob.

"Brandi?"

"Yes?" She glanced around, pinning him with a questioning look.

"I'm almost afraid to ask, but would you like a ride into

town to pick it up?" Jake felt like biting his tongue, but with the words already out it would do no good.

She stared at him, and he could almost see her mentally counting her options. "Yes, thanks."

"Four thirty?"

"I'll be ready." She closed the door without another word.

Jake flopped down into his computer chair, exhausted. Hurricane Brandi had left the building. Or at least Jake's room.

six

"Valerie!" Brandi tapped on her sister's door. "I need you."

The teen opened her door a crack, cell phone pressed to her ear. "I'm on the phone."

"That's what you said an hour ago. I have to go into town to get my car, and I need you to help Gram while I'm gone."

Valerie glared at her. "This is important."

Brandi sighed. She'd counted on Valerie's half-day school schedule to be a big help. So far her sister had spent every afternoon locked in her room. "Can you be downstairs in ten minutes?"

"Do I have a choice?"

Brandi sighed. What had happened to her adoring sister? "Not really."

Valerie closed the door in her face.

"I'll take that as a yes," Brandi muttered and hurried down to meet Jake. She would have to deal with Valerie's problem soon.

Jake stood with his back to her, looking out the front window. Much as he'd stood that night eight years ago when he'd come to pick her up. His hair had been damp then, too, curls in the back barely brushing his neck. She remembered thinking at the beginning of that night that Arkansas had some good things after all. With a jolt she realized where giving him the benefit of the doubt had gotten her then. Stranded and humiliated.

She wouldn't make the same mistake twice.

He spun around. A grin split his face, and she knew a lesser woman would have gone weak in the knees. Instead she stared at the braided rug. *Was that hand-braided?*

"You ready?"

She looked up and nodded. "Anytime."

He held the door open for her and followed her to his truck. As soon as he started the motor he tuned into a country radio station.

She should have known.

He motioned toward the radio. "Do you mind?"

She shook her head. She didn't mind, as long as she could repeat to herself over and over, "I'll have my own car back in thirty minutes."

"Are you still mad at me?" With his right hand he turned the volume down. Maybe he was more perceptive than she'd thought, both to her music tastes and her mood. But how did she respond to a question like that?

She stared out the window as she considered possible answers. *Should I be?. . .Not at all. . .Maybe a little.* Or the honest one. "Yes."

"Ouch." His dimple appeared briefly, so she wondered if he thought she was kidding.

She looked over at him and raised her eyebrows. "The truth hurts."

"So what can I do to make it up to you?"

Leave me alone? No, there was a limit to the amount of honesty a ten-minute trip could stand. And she was pretty sure she'd reached it. "Really, Jake, let's forget it. Thank you for taking care of my car."

"Why are you so afraid for someone to help you?"

"It has nothing to do with me not being willing to take help."

"Then what does it have to do with?"

She tapped the beat to the current song on her knee.

Surprisingly it wasn't half-bad. "Control. It probably has to do with control." She made a face. "Satisfied? I'm one of those control freaks you always hear about, so beware."

"I think there's a difference between being a control freak and liking to control your own destiny, for lack of a better word, in this crazy world." Jake flipped his blinker and maneuvered the truck onto the road.

She added amazing insight to her list of reasons to keep her guard up around him. Right behind finely tuned physique and killer grin. How much was a girl supposed to take?

When she didn't speak, he continued. "Don't you think God gives us a desire to think for ourselves?"

"Definitely."

One more for the list. Spiritual depth. That was unexpected and tougher to resist.

But then Mitch had seemed strong in his faith, at first. That had been the main reason she'd gone out with him. That and the fact that he was settled and steady. Something Traveling Jake, the baseball man, didn't have a clue about.

She needed stability. And she could only have that if she counted on God and herself, and no one else. She mentally shredded the list. Some things were better not thought about.

She looked at the creek as they passed smoothly over the low-water bridge. The water down below rippled cheerfully. Not a hint remained of the dangerous monster within.

"It sure looks different, doesn't it?" Jake asked quietly.

She nodded. If the list hadn't been lying in tiny imaginary shredded strips on the floor, she'd have been forced to add sensitive to it.

When she didn't speak for a few minutes, he eased the radio volume up slightly. She stared out the window until they reached town. It hadn't changed a bit. At least on the outside. Same psychedelic painted flower shop. Same full-service gas station. The pizza parlor sign still touted "MADE FRESH DAILY" as their claim to fame. She'd always wondered who would buy day-old pizza.

In spite of its idiosyncrasies the town seemed to suck the next generation of residents easily into its swirling vortex of sameness. Les operated his dad's towing business. Dana had opened a beauty shop on Main Street. Quentin worked for his brother at the mechanic shop. Brandi had been lucky to escape.

"Whatever happened to Elizabeth Battlestone?" Elizabeth had been one of her few friends. Mostly because she always had her nose stuck in a book, so she was harassed by the other girls almost as much as Brandi was. Before Jake answered, Brandi saw the library sign. No doubt Elizabeth was in there, cataloguing books.

"She's an award-winning Christian novelist. She writes under her married name—Elizabeth Campbell—but you can find her books in most any bookstore."

"Really? I think I've seen her books." So much for Brandi's theory. "So she moved away, too." Who could blame her after the way Tammy and the other girls had treated her?

"No. She still lives here. She's on the city council and is president of Friends of the Library. She married Steve Campbell, a buddy of mine from college. They own a successful computer software company off Main Street."

"An award-winning novelist lives here?" *And the owner of a computer software company?*

"Along with an Olympic gold medalist and a pro-baseball player." His self-deprecatory grin belied the proud words.

Brandi thought of adding famous model to his list of noteworthy locals, but if he chose not to mention Tammy, why should she? "Olympic gold medalist?"

"Yeah, didn't you know Mr. Johnson won a gold medal for

swimming before he started teaching agriculture?"

She shook her head. Somehow during her brief time in the seemingly inconsequential Arkansas town, Mr. Johnson's claim to fame had eluded her.

Jake nodded toward the coffee shop. "Of course, there are our most famous residents. Or at least they should be."

"The domino players?" Brandi grinned. It was amazing how differently two people could look at one town.

"Yep. The recipients of at least a dozen Purple Hearts and half a dozen Congressional Medals of Honor are sitting in there at those tables."

"Wow. I'm impressed." Brandi said it in a teasing tone, but she was. To her core.

"It's about time." He smiled.

"Maybe I'll look up Elizabeth since she's still in town."

"I know she'd be glad. She asks your parents about you all the time. Haven't they ever mentioned it to you?" Brandi shook her head. She hated to tell him she'd made it clear to her mom and dad years ago that she didn't want to hear anything about Arkansas. She breathed a sigh of relief when the auto shop came into view.

"Here we are." Jake grinned and whipped his truck into the parking lot and killed the motor. "Let's go get your wheels so you can be in control."

She blushed. "Lead the way."

ॐ

A car door slammed. Jake pushed back from the computer and rubbed his eyes with his fingers. Time for a seventh-inning stretch. He stood and walked to the window.

In the driveway below Brandi retrieved blue plastic grocery bags from the convertible trunk and passed them to Michael and Melissa. The threesome's easy camaraderie was evident, even though he couldn't hear their words. When both kids had several bags, Brandi grabbed the rest and slammed the trunk. With her hair up in a high ponytail, she didn't look much older than Michael.

It had been over a week since Jake had taken Brandi into town to pick up her car. Almost everything in the car had been salvageable, so he'd helped her carry her things up to her room that day. She'd thanked him, but he could count on one hand the number of words they'd exchanged since then. Why he kept trying to get through to her, he really didn't know. Changing her attitude toward Arkansas— toward him—represented a challenge. And Jake could never resist a challenge.

When he was young he'd been determined to prove he was more than just the baby brother of the McFadden boys. So every test that came his way he jumped into it with both feet, and he had the scars to prove it. That hadn't stopped teachers from comparing him to Cade, Holt, or Clint, but at least his peers knew he was an individual in his own right.

His natural talent for baseball had given him a good way out of his brothers' larger-than-life shadows in high school. By the time he'd reached college he'd found another way. Playing the rebel. Wild parties became the normal way to spend a weekend. He hadn't figured out it wasn't a game until it was too late.

He slapped the desk. The best thing he could do right now was get out of this room for a while. Away from bad memories, plummeting Web site stats, and fears that he would never recover.

❧

After two weeks of preparation Brandi would be welcoming her first overnight guests to the B&B in a few hours. She was probably frantic trying to get everything ready. Maybe he should help.

He could hear Brandi calling Valerie's name as he stepped

into the hall. On second thought maybe he should stay out of the way and let her take care of it herself.

As he passed Valerie's door, it burst open.

"I said I'll be there in a minute!" Valerie screamed, practically in his ear.

Her red face turned ashen when she saw him. "Jake. I'm sorry. I didn't see you there."

"Hey, no problem. I have another ear." He smiled at the girl who had practically been a ray of sunshine until a few weeks ago. "I've missed seeing you at meals. Everything okay?"

She shook her head, and tears filled her eyes. "I guess."

"Rough time at school, huh?"

She nodded.

"Want to talk about it?"

"Not right now, but thanks."

"If you ever change your mind, I do have one good ear left." He spied a stack of blank B&B guest comment cards on a nearby table. He quickly jotted down his cell phone number on one and handed it to her.

A smile flitted across her face. "Thanks. I'll remember that."

After Valerie closed her door, Jake said a silent prayer for her. She needed to talk to someone soon. Brandi would be the logical choice, but Valerie would have to come to that realization on her own. Even though reaching out to troubled teens came naturally to him, Jake was through interfering in Miss California's life.

He could hear Brandi barking orders to Michael and Melissa as he walked quietly down the stairs. The foyer was empty. Ducking his head a little, he eased the door open and slipped out onto the porch.

The first hint of autumn crispness filled the air. He took a deep breath. The slight breeze carried a fragrance of peace and sunshine that chased away his earlier doubts about pitching again. The Creator had outdone Himself.

"There's nothing like the first real day of autumn, is there?" Jake jumped then smiled.

Elva had stretched out on a chaise lounge at one end of the long porch with an open book on her knees.

"Nothing at all," he agreed.

"I have to rest on the ice pack for twenty minutes and do some crunches." She closed the book and laid it beside her on the porch. "I couldn't bear another second of that room."

"I know what you mean," Jake said. "My walls were closing in, too." He walked over and sat in the rocker nearest Elva's chair.

"It's hard for me to be here and not be able to help Brandi," Elva said. She raised her knees up and repositioned. "I tried to tell her this old house has been receiving guests for so long it could almost do it on its own. But she didn't listen."

"You sound like you've known this house longer than eight years."

"Yes, my sister owned it for forty years and ran it, first as a boardinghouse and later as a B&B. When she died, I inherited it." She wrinkled her nose. "I had no desire to leave my home, but Tom and Lynette were thrilled about the idea of running the B&B and making a home for their four children."

She raised her head, tightening her muscles, then relaxed. "They'd lived with me since my husband had died, and I hated to see them go, but I knew it would be perfect for them. And it was." Elva focused on Jake again as if she'd been lost in the past for a few minutes.

"They seem to have really made a home here," Jake said. Not very many people loved as unselfishly as Elva had, giving up seeing her kids and grandkids regularly, so they could be happy.

"Yes, they do, don't they?" She smiled. "I'm thankful God blessed them with this. They needed roots, but it took some time for them to find their place. Everything happens in its own time." She waved her hand toward the house. "But right now Brandi's in a tizzy about the guests coming, and there's not a thing I can say to calm her down."

"She strikes me as the type who needs to do things her way." Jake mentally patted himself on the back. Considering she seemed like a borderline control freak at times, he deserved a gold star for that tactful understatement.

Elva snickered. "You know her pretty well."

Jake rocked slowly without speaking. Even though he wished it were otherwise, nothing could be further from the truth.

Almost as if she read his mind, Elva continued. "Brandi had never lived more than a year in one place when her family moved into my house after Sam's death. She was going into the eighth grade. Every day for the next four years she blossomed." She motioned toward the morning sun. "Consistency was her sunlight. Moving her here right before her senior year turned her life upside down way more than any of us realized it would. After that, I think she decided she would never allow herself to be vulnerable to someone else's decisions."

"That must have made for a lonely life." His heart went out to the little girl, longing for a home then having to leave the one she finally had.

"It seems like every time she's let her guard down, she's been hurt. So I guess she figures lonely is worth it as long as she's safe."

Jake remembered Brandi's caustic attitude in high school. Had that been a defense mechanism? A protective wall?

"Now, if you'll help an old lady up from here, my twenty

minutes are up, and I'll leave you to enjoy this beautiful day in peace."

Jake gently lifted her to her feet and said good-bye. After she went in, he remained in the rocker, thinking about what she'd said. Brandi needed to trust someone enough to consciously put herself in that person's hands. Until that happened, she didn't have a chance at happiness.

He grimaced. Who was he to psychoanalyze someone else's life when he couldn't even manage his own?

seven

"Can you believe it's really over?" Brandi could hear the triumph in her voice, but she couldn't help it. She'd been so nervous.

Valerie laughed. "Another day, another dollar."

"Yeah, it's old hat to you, but to me, surviving our first night with guests and getting them all safely tucked into bed is a victory."

"Tucked into bed?" Valerie looked up from the magazines she was straightening and raised an eyebrow.

"Figuratively speaking, of course. But I did hear you offer to read a bedtime story to the five-year-old in the WIZARD OF OZ suite."

"Well, the little squirt wasn't going to settle down if I didn't, especially after her mom let her have that extra helping of chocolate pudding at supper."

"Good point. I should have known you weren't being nice for no reason," Brandi teased.

"Me? Never." Although her words were said in the same teasing tone Brandi had used, something that looked like pain crossed Valerie's face.

"Thanks for being so much help tonight. If you want to go on to bed, I can finish up here."

The teen shook her head. "It'll go faster if we both do it." She picked up a doll and dropped it into the toy basket.

Brandi stared at her sister's back. Valerie had been a little sullen when she first came down, but for the past ten hours she'd been back to her old self. Brandi couldn't fathom what had brought about the change, but she wasn't complaining.

She checked the reservation book to be sure she didn't need to leave any special diet instructions for Nellie.

Valerie ran the cordless sweeper back and forth on the rug then looked up as if struck by a sudden thought. "Oh, Angie and Brit are going to Batesville to the movie in a little while. They're going to pick me up in about fifteen minutes."

Brandi looked at her watch. "At ten o'clock?"

"Yeah, the theater's trying something new this summer. A late, late show."

"How can you do that and still be home by midnight?"

Valerie's face reddened. "Well, I was hoping since we'd worked so late, you'd cut me some slack on the curfew. I should be home by two. Two thirty at the latest."

"Valerie! Tomorrow's church. And besides that, you know I can't just ditch your curfew. Mom and Dad set that back when I was in high school."

"That proves how out of date it is."

Brandi cringed.

Valerie narrowed her eyes. "You're in charge now, remember? You can change it if you want to."

"I'm sorry." She reached over to touch her sister's shoulder, but she shrugged away. "Not tonight. If this late, late movie is going to be a regular thing at the cinema, we'll ask Mom and Dad about it next time they call."

Valerie's eyes filled with tears. "Sometimes it's hard to believe you're my sister. You don't understand anything at all." She stomped from the room.

Brandi slid into the chair and closed her eyes. She probably should have handled that differently. Maybe she should have offered to go, too, and drive the girls. She hated to be a drag. Being a parent figure wasn't as easy as it looked.

She stood to her feet and went from room to room turning

out the main lights. Some guests couldn't resist tiptoeing down to the kitchen for a midnight snack. In anticipation of their nocturnal wanderings, automatic nightlights bathed the downstairs in a soft golden glow.

Suddenly an oatmeal raisin cookie and a mug of milk seemed like just what Brandi needed to smooth away the sharp edges of hurt that Valerie's tirade had left on her heart. *Comfort food, take me away.*

She tiptoed to the kitchen and pushed open the door.

Jake McFadden sat at the counter, a big glass of milk in front of him, a cookie in his hand. He smiled. "You caught me."

She pushed her hair away from her face and sank down onto a stool. "Actually I was about to do the same thing. That's not the last cookie, is it?"

He slid the cookie jar across to her and smoothly slipped a cup off the mug tree. In seconds she had a plate with three cookies and a cup full of milk in front of her.

"Thanks."

"You're welcome. How'd it go today? You seemed to do a great job of handling the guests."

"It went well. I was pretty nervous, but Valerie helped so much. So did Michael and Melissa, but they disappeared right after supper."

"I think Michael is working on a new invention. And of course he couldn't do much without his able assistant."

"Of course not. Oh, well, I gave them permission to be excused, so I wasn't complaining." She dunked her cookie into her milk in what she hoped was a discreet move. "But Valerie stuck it out to the end."

"She really seemed like her old self tonight."

She swallowed her bite of cookie and frowned. "Yeah, until a few minutes ago."

"Everything okay?"

"She wanted to go out, and I said no."

"At ten o'clock at night?" Jake's incredulous tone made Brandi feel better. She'd wondered if she was completely out of touch.

"Yeah, to a late, late show, but she said she'd be in by two thirty at the latest." Brandi rolled her eyes.

Jake chuckled. "She must have thought you were an easy mark to try to get away with that."

Brandi looked at his smile, and her heart lifted a little. He had a way of putting things into perspective. "I guess. But now I'm the 'wicked witch of the West.'" She sipped her milk. "Just like Tammy and her friends used to call me."

Jake looked startled, and Brandi immediately regretted her words. She shouldn't have brought up the past. She'd grown up enough to know that often kids are cruel to other kids. Just because he'd gone along with it then didn't make him a bad person now. After all, he'd saved her life. That should cover a lot of instances of poor judgment on his part.

"Tammy called you that?"

She made a face. "Don't tell me you don't remember."

He shook his head.

"You know how they were. They were never so obvious as to flat out call me names, but they would write WWOTW on my notebooks and papers when I wasn't looking or whisper the initials in their conversations when I walked by."

"How did you know that's what it stood for?"

She met his gaze and was surprised to see true puzzlement in the depth of his dark blue eyes. "The first time or two they wrote it, I had no idea; so when she knew I was listening, Tammy glanced at my notebook then turned to one of her friends and made some comment about the most vile movie character being the 'wicked witch of the West.'" Brandi looked down at the counter and concentrated on a tiny nick in its surface. "She said the words very slowly with emphasis on each one. I guess she thought I was stupid."

Jake set his cup down. "It's hard for me to believe Tammy would do that."

Brandi jerked her head up. Did he think she was making it up? All this time she'd assumed he'd known Tammy's true nature and overlooked it because she was beautiful.

"Well, she did. And her friends did, too." She sounded like a petulant child. She smiled to take the sting out of her affirmation. "I don't blame them anymore. My anger about being in Arkansas made me an easy target."

He didn't speak.

She pushed to her feet. "I'm sorry I brought this up. I hope you don't think I was attacking Tammy. I know you two stayed close after school."

She had actually seen a picture of him and the gorgeous brunette in a magazine last year during baseball season. The caption had called her Tami, which Brandi assumed was her professional name. Brandi and Krista had joked about how typical it was of her to try to steal Brandi's "i" instead of being happy with the "y" she was born with. Since Jake never mentioned her name now—either spelling—Brandi assumed they were history.

He stood, brow furrowed. "I'm just wondering how I could have missed something like that. I'm sorry for not seeing it and standing up for you."

She smiled. "That's okay." She remembered Tammy's glittering eyes the night of Dana's party. "I think it would have been worse for me if you had." She rinsed out her cup and put it in the dishwasher then turned around to face him again. "Good night, Jake. Sweet dreams."

"You, too."

She left him sitting at the counter staring into his coffee

mug as if the secrets of the universe were unfolding in his milk.

≈

Jake pulled his pillow over his head and slapped his hand toward the alarm clock. Where was that snooze button? The persistent noise invaded his sleep. He caught the clock square on and hit it hard. The noise kept on. He knocked the pillow off and sat up. The lighted dial of his cell phone made it easy to find. He picked it up and pushed the button. "Hello?"

"Jake. It's Valerie!" The frantic whisper chased away the last of the sleep fog. He blinked and focused on the red numbers of his alarm clock. 3:00 a.m.?

"Valerie?"

"You know how you said if I ever wanted to talk. . . ." Her voice sounded thick with tears.

"Yes." Only a teenager would call him from twenty feet down the hall in the middle of the night.

"Well, I need to talk now. But first I need you to come get me."

Uh oh. "Where are you?"

"I'm at the edge of the Rainey woods. Do you know where that is?"

"Sure. What are you doing there?" Jake jumped up and grabbed his jeans off the chair. He shrugged into them as she spoke.

"There was a party in the clearing." *Sniff.* "I climbed out my window, and Angie and Brit picked me up." *Sniff.* "But now they've gone off with their boyfriends and left me, and I thought I liked this guy, but now I don't. . .and I just want to come home." The sniffs dissolved into full-blown sobs.

He pulled a T-shirt over his head. "Okay, calm down. Is anyone else with you?"

"I'm hiding."

"Hiding?" He slipped on his tennis shoes without socks. "Tell me exactly where you are."

"I'm behind the big oak closest to the gravel road. It has some sort of deer stand in it."

"I know it. I'll get Brandi, and we'll be right there."

"No! Please don't tell her."

Jake froze. "Valerie, I have to. She's your guardian right now, and she loves you. You can't keep this a secret from her."

"I'll tell her in the morning. I promise. Just please come get me."

Jake grabbed a windbreaker jacket. By the time he woke Brandi, it could cost crucial seconds. They could sort this out in the morning. In the meantime Valerie needed him. "I'll be there in a few minutes."

"Hurry."

"Do you want me to stay on the phone with you while I'm driving over there?"

"No, my battery's about to go dead. I'll call you back if I need to."

"Okay. Stay hidden, Valerie. I'll see you soon."

"Hurry, Jake. Please?"

He disconnected the phone and slipped out of his room into the hall. He tiptoed across the hardwood floor, wincing as the fourth stair from the bottom creaked. He wished he had time to wake up Brandi, regardless of what the teen wanted. But right now Valerie's safety had to be his top priority. Surely Brandi would understand that.

When he was in his truck, he prayed for God to keep Valerie safe and to give Brandi an understanding heart. After he finished, he thought again of the accusations Brandi had made against Tammy and her crowd. He wanted to deny it, even to himself, but in the pit of his stomach he knew she was telling the truth.

Tammy had occasionally shown a streak of cruelty over the years. She'd honed in on his weaknesses and fears, throwing them up to him during arguments. Jake had tried to excuse her by blaming it on her father's leaving when she was little. Insecurity, low self-esteem. But those excuses didn't make her actions acceptable.

He wondered if subconsciously that facet of her personality had kept him from trying to take their relationship to the next level. Because, even though his family thought Tammy's career had stood in the way of a permanent arrangement between the two, the truth was Jake had never asked her to marry him. And he'd never been able to put his finger on why.

Whatever the reason, he was well rid of his ties to her. And to his surprise, since he'd recovered some from the blow to his pride, his heart appeared to be barely scathed by her betrayal.

He could bump himself for not seeing her true nature sooner, though. No wonder Brandi had been so defensive in school. Heat suffused his face in the dark vehicle. He had called her Miss That's-not-how-we-do-it-in-California because he'd thought she was infuriatingly superior-acting. Tammy wasn't the only one who'd been unfair to her.

Lost in the past he almost didn't recognize the big oak. At the last minute he pulled onto the dirt turnoff that led back into the woods that surrounded the legendary clearing. Kids had been getting into mischief here for as long as he could remember.

A lone figure darted from behind the tree and yanked his truck door open. When she was safely inside, she pulled the door shut, her breath coming in ragged gasps.

"Did anyone hurt you?"

"No." Valerie grimaced. "Just my feelings."

"Those are important." He couldn't stop the relief that flowed through him, though.

He tossed her the same hunting coat Brandi had used the day of the flood. She took it and wrapped it around her.

The silence on the trip home was punctuated only by Valerie's sniffles. But Jake knew from his work with teens that he couldn't stay quiet. As much as he hated to bombard Valerie with questions, he needed to be sure of some things before he let her wait until morning to tell Brandi.

He eased the truck into the B&B parking lot and turned to face her. "Valerie, if you've had drugs or alcohol tonight, we need to wake Brandi right now and let her know."

She gave a half-choked laugh. "No, my life is complicated enough right now without any help. I'm totally sober. I promise."

He studied her tear-streaked face by the glow of the guard light. His gut said she was telling the truth. In lieu of a lie detector test he was going with his gut.

He looked up at Brandi's dark window then back at Valerie. "Okay, let's go in quietly. You need to get to bed." He doubted seriously if he'd be able to go back to sleep. This secret rescue mission stood to undo all the progress he and Brandi had made in the kitchen tonight, and for some reason that thought bothered him more than he cared to admit.

They walked in silence up the sidewalk. He pulled out the key Tom Delaney had given him when he first checked in. Before he could get it into the lock, the door swung open.

Brandi stood in the foyer, her robe clutched around her. She stared at him and Valerie. Angry tears glittered in her eyes. "Good morning. Glad you two finally made it home."

eight

Jake took a step back. Surely Brandi didn't believe for a second that he and Valerie had been slipping out together for a late-night rendezvous. "Brandi, let me explain."

"Let's see." Brandi began to tick off statements on her fingers. "Valerie snuck out her window, got into some kind of trouble, called you, and you put on your shining armor and flew off to the rescue without a thought of telling me. And now you're both congratulating yourself for putting one over on the mean big sister. Does that about sum it up?" Her tone was flat and low.

Valerie put her hands on hips. "No! You're not being fair. I was going to tell you first thing in the morning. As far as that goes, I would have told you before I went if you weren't so. . . ." Valerie words sputtered away as Brandi drew herself up to her full height and stared down at her little sister.

Jake stared at Valerie, too. Was this the same penitent girl he'd picked up in the woods?

He turned to face Brandi. "I had to hurry, but before I agreed to go get her, Valerie promised she would tell you—"

Brandi gave him a cutting glance. "You know what? I don't even care about your part in this." She looked back at Valerie whose tears had resurfaced after her momentary bravado. To Jake's surprise a veil of tenderness blended with the anger on Brandi's face. "Val. You okay?"

Valerie nodded.

"I found your window open, and I was worried sick. I can't believe you crawled down that drainpipe."

Valerie threw herself into her sister's arms, fresh tears streaking down her face. Brandi smoothed Valerie's hair with a trembling hand and pinned Jake with a glare. "Taking over my car's restoration and taking over my sister's safety are two different things. You need to learn to stay out of things that don't concern you."

"And you need to realize you can't be in control of every situation, no matter how hard you try." Jake couldn't keep from feeling a twinge of anger. How had he suddenly become the bad guy? "Valerie called *me*."

"I'm sorry, Brandi," Valerie whispered. "I should have called you to come get me."

Jake narrowed his eyes. He knew Valerie was sorry for slipping out, but how much of this was a calculated act to get out of trouble?

"I understand, honey. Jake sees himself as the hero in every situation." Even though she was speaking to the girl she held tight, Brandi's glittering eyes bore into his. "Subconsciously you probably bought into that."

Jake snorted. "Give a guy a break." Irritation combined with little sleep had his temper on edge. "I'm going to bed. You know what? Forget it. I'm getting out of here." He brushed past the sisters and hurried to his room.

This was definitely the last time he tried to help the Delaney sisters.

&

Brandi closed her door and leaned against it. As far as she knew, until a few weeks ago her sister had been a model student and a seemingly committed Christian. Was it coincidence that the minute Brandi was in charge Valerie became a juvenile delinquent wanna-be?

Brandi had tucked the repentant teen into bed with the admonishment that she *would* get up in two hours for church, regardless of how tired she was. A late-night party in the woods did *not* constitute a good reason to miss worship. By the time Brandi left the room, Valerie was sprawled across the bed, dead to the world.

And now Brandi was hiding in her room trying to muster up the strength to face the day. Where was the fairness in that? She still had to dole out Valerie's punishment, whatever that should be, and deal pleasantly with guests. And then, if that weren't enough, Jake's "I'm getting out of here" had sounded suspiciously final. Had he meant he was moving out?

She peeked out the window. His truck was gone. That empty parking place made her stomach feel as if she'd swallowed a live octopus. She was furious about his actions tonight, and she despised the unpredictable lifestyle he was fighting so hard to get back to, but it would be hard to imagine the B&B without him.

She grabbed her Bible and threw herself across her bed on her stomach. She opened it to the book of Philippians and forced herself to concentrate on the words. She'd gotten halfway through chapter four yesterday, but she only had time for two or three verses this morning. But whatever they were she needed them desperately.

Her eyes fell on the words at the end of verse eleven. *For I have learned, in whatsoever state I am, therewith to be content.* Brandi grimaced. She knew the apostle Paul didn't mean "state" as in United States of America, but ever since she'd moved in with her parents when she was seventeen, she hadn't been able to read this verse without guilt. She hadn't been content in Arkansas by any stretch of the imagination. It was more bearable this time, so maybe she was learning. She remembered the scene with Valerie and Jake. Or maybe not.

She closed her eyes and let her face fall down on the Bible.

Lord, I need Your strength today. I'm confused. Help me deal with Val in the right way. And Michael and Melissa, too. And even Jake. If he comes back. Thank You for never letting me down. And thank You for Your Son. In His name I pray. Amen.

Two more verses and then she had to get a shower and dress. After she read verse twelve and started thirteen, she stopped. Of course. Philippians 4:13. Her favorite verse. She'd been so brain-dead from no sleep that she hadn't even realized it was next. *I can do all things through Christ which strengtheneth me.*

Amen.

She laid her Bible on the nightstand and headed to the shower, considerably more lighthearted. After she dressed, she tiptoed downstairs to Gram's room and tapped on the door. Following her time with God, Brandi felt better than she had since her car washed off the bridge; but the fact remained that she'd been here a little over a week and she was already messing up her sister's life and chasing away guests. It was time to seek Gram's wise advice.

"Come in."

Brandi eased the door open. Her grandmother lay on the bed, knees bent, with an ice pack on her back.

"Hi, Gram. How's it going?" Brandi crossed the room and hugged her gently.

"I'm better. But I'm aggravated that I can't be more help."

"Just knowing you're here helps me. Can I talk to you for a few minutes?"

Gram patted the bed. "Sit down and tell me what's on your mind."

Brandi perched beside her and poured out her heart to the older woman. When she finished, she waited for Gram's advice.

"Honey, we need to pray."

Brandi didn't tell her she'd already done that because Gram's prayers always made Brandi think of crawling up into the

Father's lap and telling Him her problems. She bowed her head as Gram brought their concerns to God. Even though she felt tears damp on her cheeks, peace seeped into her soul.

"Jake will be back," Gram said softly. "He's not one to run away when the going gets tough. Quite the opposite."

"Well, it doesn't matter that much. I just hate to lose a permanent guest for the B&B."

Gram didn't reply, but her piercing gaze made Brandi's face grow hot.

"Really, my main worry is Valerie."

"Valerie's going to come through this fine with time and prayers. I'm sure you remember it's not easy being a teenager." Gram patted her hand.

Brandi nodded. That was an understatement.

&

"Jake, are you sure you don't want another piece of apple pie?" Megan McFadden asked. She sounded nonchalant, but Jake didn't miss the concerned look that passed between his sister-in-law and brother.

Jake shook his head. "No, thanks. It was delicious, though." Megan apparently thought whatever ailed him could be cured by filling his stomach. She'd been offering him food ever since he showed up unannounced on their doorstep this morning. He'd eaten a big breakfast with them before going to church and had just inhaled a man-sized lunch.

"You look as if you could use a nap," his brother Holt offered. "Why don't you try out my hammock while I help Megan with the dishes?"

"Now that sounds like an offer I can't refuse. I didn't get much sleep last night."

"Did you have a bad dream, Uncle Jake?" asked Sarah, his eight-year-old niece. She handed him a drawing she'd been working on since lunch.

"Not really. Just a lot of interruptions." He thought about the fiery anger in Brandi's eyes. Forcing the memory from his mind he studied the incredible rendering of Sarah's family, including her golden retriever, Rascal, and her uncle Jake. "Honey, what a beautiful picture! Thank you. I feel better already." He held the paper up to show Megan and Holt.

Sarah threw her arms around his neck. "C'mon, and I'll show you the hammock. We got it for Daddy for Father's Day."

As Jake followed Sarah outside, he thought of how his brother's life had changed since he'd married Megan and adopted Sarah. The Arkansas Senate's most eligible—and most stressed—bachelor was now a relaxed, easygoing dad and husband. And an even better senator, to boot.

A few minutes later Jake stretched out in the hammock and closed his eyes. Sarah stood on tiptoes and dropped a kiss on his cheek. "I'm going to play with Rascal. See you after awhile."

"Have fun," Jake murmured and surrendered to the deep weariness in his bones. Dappled shadows danced across his closed eyelids, as sunlight played hide-and-seek through the trees.

Brandi Delaney was incredibly stubborn. And incredibly fascinating.

He opened his eyes then shut them again quickly as a ray of sunlight found its target. He had to stop thinking of the beautiful blond every time he got still. She definitely wasn't his problem.

He thought back to Elva's words when they were out on the porch. With all the turmoil she'd had in her upbringing, Brandi needed a California man with a nine-to-five job who would give her a house on the beach and a stable life. Not a baseball player who lived more on the road than anywhere else.

He clutched the woven rope web and turned onto his side

then pulled the hammock pillow over his eyes. Why was he contemplating the future of a girl he barely knew? All this domesticity was pickling his brain.

Something cold on his arm brought him back from a dream about a girl in a red convertible that kept driving off every time he got close to her. He didn't have to be Freud to figure that one out. He opened his eyes. Rascal was licking him as if he were a big ice cream cone. Sarah stood by watching quietly.

"I didn't want to wake you up, but Rascal did. He wants you to play with us."

Jake smiled and looked at his watch. He'd slept for two hours. He yawned and patted the dog's head. "Let's play some ball, Rascal."

As Jake threw the tennis ball for the tenth time, his brother walked across the yard.

"Glad to see you're keeping in practice," Holt called.

"I have to unless I want to go back to being just Senator Holt McFadden's little brother," Jake teased.

"Somehow I don't think that's your reason for playing ball." Holt smiled. "Let's see—money, fame. . . ." He counted them on his fingers. "Have I left out anything?"

"Yeah, the biggest thing." Jake ran his fingers through his hair.

"Your chance to speak out against drugs in high schools." Holt's smile fled.

"Yep." He looked over at Holt. "I get tired of being on the road all the time." He motioned toward the house and Sarah. "And a big part of me would love to settle down and have a family. Coach football and baseball at a small town school. But it's worth the hassles in order to help kids say no to drugs and alcohol."

"When are you going to forgive yourself for the accident?"

Holt's normally level tone was exasperated.

"I've forgiven myself. Everyone makes mistakes," Jake said. Forgiving wasn't the same as forgetting, but his family loved him and wanted to erase his past.

"You could still travel around and speak to schools even if you're not able to stay on the team."

Jake shook his head. "People have short memories. Since I've been out this season, the visits to my Web site have cut almost in half. I have to do both or neither."

Holt shrugged. "Well, then you could quit and coach, as you said. You have the degree. Think how much influence your coaches had on you."

Jake's mouth twisted into a rueful grin. "Apparently not enough."

"Maybe not that one year. But you know the rest of the time your coaches had a big impact on you."

"I know. But I'm going back to baseball." No one knew the deals Jake had made with himself in order to crawl up from the pits of despair. "And the road trips go with it."

"Is that what happened to you and Tammy? Your road trips?"

Jake knew his family wondered. But he hadn't been ready to talk about it. For some reason he didn't mind all that much now. "Yes and no."

" 'Zat right?" Holt deadpanned.

"She didn't mind me being on the road." Jake took the tennis ball from the prancing golden retriever and flung it across the yard with his left hand. "Turns out that gave her the perfect opportunity to get to know other men better."

"Oh, man. I'm sorry."

"Yeah, well, she didn't want to break it off. But that was something I wasn't 'hip' enough to accept. So I told her it was over." The dog brought the ball back, and Jake obligingly threw it again then wiped his hand on his pants. "She still leaves messages—but I don't return her calls. Instead I'm concentrating on getting my career back."

They stood in silence and watched Sarah and Rascal chase each other. "Whether you make it back or not, there's more to you than just baseball, Jake. And there's more than one way to make a difference."

Jake nodded. He'd never doubted his family loved him and was proud of him whether he played pro-ball or not. But he wasn't willing to give up a chance to motivate thousands of teens to say no to drugs. Not after what he'd done.

"So what's keeping you up nights these days?" Holt gestured toward the hammock.

Jake groaned. "Brandi Delaney."

"Tom and Lynette's daughter?"

"Yep, straight from California and proud of it."

"Wasn't she in your class?" Holt asked.

"Yeah, my senior year. She was my one try at dating someone besides Tammy. Needless to say it didn't work out."

"I remember. You were intrigued by her. Are you two—"

"Please! Not a chance. She drives me crazy."

Holt threw back his head and laughed. "I hate to tell you this, bro, but that's exactly how it starts."

nine

" 'Bye, Mr. Cline. Come back and see us." When the door closed behind the last of her Tuesday night guests, Brandi turned her attention to the Wednesday page of the reservation book.

A businessman from Washington and two couples on their way to Branson from Florida were on the schedule for tonight, but they wouldn't arrive for a few more hours. The house was quiet with only her, Nellie, and Gram here.

Jake had been gone since the wee hours of Sunday morning. Four days counting today. She thought sure he'd have been back by now. Unless he wasn't coming back.

Sunday she'd still been mad so she hadn't cared as much. She'd looked for him at church though. He hadn't been there.

She found out Monday afternoon from Valerie that the frightened girl had begged Jake to hurry to get her and promised to tell Brandi Sunday morning. He'd most likely acted quickly out of concern for Val's safety. After this confirmation that she'd overreacted to Jake's part in the whole thing she felt even worse about his departure.

By yesterday she was replaying every hateful thing she'd said. She didn't sleep much last night. And all morning she'd been remembering his saving her life, even though he had a hurt shoulder. He could have just called 911.

Brandi opened the safety box and looped Mr. Cline's key onto the second hook in a row of six. Her gaze fell on the extra key to Jake's room. Maybe she should just peek in and see if all his things were gone.

Before she could talk herself out of it she slipped the gold key into her pocket. If he were gone for good, she'd rather know now. She was halfway up the stairs when she heard Gram call from the den.

She jumped. "Yes?"

"I'm going to go now."

"Go?" Brandi muttered and retraced her steps. When she saw Gram, she let out a low whistle. "Mama mia! You look nice."

"Thank you." Gram beamed.

"How are you feeling?"

"Better." She waved her cane. "Dr. Barnes says I'll still need this for a while. But I'm improving. That's what I was going to tell you. I have a chiropractic appointment."

"Do you want me to drive you?" Brandi offered automatically, even though Gram had refused her the other times.

"Thanks, but no. I have my lumbar cushion, and as long as I'm able I want to drive myself."

Brandi wondered if stubborn independence ran in the family. She took another look at Gram. In that red pants outfit she looked like a movie star. "You're just going to the *chiropractor*?"

The older woman chuckled. "I don't think I said I was *just* going to the chiropractor. Actually I'm meeting Ben for lunch afterward."

"Ben Carter? *Coach* Carter?"

"Don't sound so shocked. It's not very flattering to know you think I'm too old to have a life."

Brandi laughed. "Hardly. You're the youngest granny I know. So don't get too attached to that cane."

"I won't." Gram dropped a kiss on Brandi's cheek and left.

The door closed, and Brandi took a deep breath. Back to her mission. If she didn't get that key out of her pocket soon, it might self-destruct. Or her guilt might make *her* self-destruct.

She was strung tighter than a fiddler's bow.

Brandi's foot had touched the top stair when the front door burst open. "Yii!" she screamed and spun around.

Valerie blasted into the house, thrusting her book bag in front of her. She raised an eyebrow. "What's wrong with you?"

Brandi concentrated on making her breathing even. "Oh, nothing. You're home early."

"Yeah, I ditched my last class."

It was Brandi's turn to raise an eyebrow, but since her eye was still twitching from the shock of the door bursting open, she settled for pursing her lips in disbelief and shaking her head.

"I'm kidding. We had an optional assembly right before lunch. So I came on home." Valerie smiled. Not overly friendly, but not hostile at least.

Brandi had made Valerie call their parents yesterday and let them decide what her punishment would be. Being restricted from both her cell phone and the house phone, plus the television and computer, hadn't improved Valerie's disposition. And being confined to the house except for school for two weeks was going to leave her with some time on her hands.

"Your chore list is on the reception table."

"I can hardly wait." Valerie pushed her bag ahead of her up the stairs. "I've got to put my book bag in my room."

Brandi touched the key through her jeans pocket. She might as well go talk to Nellie about tonight's menu.

Ten minutes later, when Brandi came from the kitchen, Valerie was at the front door carrying the trash out to the Dumpster.

Quiet again. She wiped her sweaty palms on her jeans and pulled the key from her pocket. She couldn't believe she was actually doing this. Her heart thundered in her throat when she reached Jake's door. Would all his personal belongings be gone?

Holding her breath she slid the key into the lock and opened the door. Horror shot through her veins.

Jake looked up from his desk, puzzlement written on his brow. "Brandi? Is everything all right?"

Floor, please just open up and swallow me, right now.

"Yes, um. . . ." *Think, Brandi, think.*

"Are you sure you're okay?" Jake stood, alarm in his eyes. "You look pale. Do you need to sit down?"

No, what I need is a logical excuse for unlocking your door. "No, I'm okay." She leaned against the doorframe, pretending to strike a casual pose but in reality trying to keep her knees from folding under her. "I can't believe I opened your door."

Jake waved off her words. "Don't worry about it. I'm sure you had a lot on your mind and opened the wrong door by mistake."

Now she knew. Jake McFadden was a true hero. He had provided her with the perfect excuse for her breaking and entering. She could just walk right out of this humiliating situation without so much as a backward glance.

Except it wasn't true. A year of putting up with Tammy's faux sweetness had left a bad taste in Brandi's mouth for anything that involved hiding behind a false front. And to this day she couldn't do it.

"The truth is. . . ." She stood up straight and kept her gaze locked on a spot over his shoulder. Telling him was one thing. Facing his reaction was another. "I was afraid you'd left for good. So I was just going to open your door and see if your personal things were gone."

She pressed her palm against her burning face. She felt sure there was nothing pale about it now. "I'm sorry for invading your privacy, Jake."

She averted her eyes to the floor until she heard him chuckle. "Don't you think you're being a little hard on yourself?" His blue eyes sparkled. "Checking to be sure I hadn't moved out without informing the management surely wouldn't be invasion of privacy."

"I appreciate your being so understanding. While I'm apologizing, I might as well get it all out." She glanced down and saw the key still in her hand. When he followed her gaze and smiled, she stuffed it in her pocket then looked back up at him. "I'm sorry for coming down so hard on you for helping Valerie. I know you were just worried about her."

Jake held up his hand. "Let's don't go overboard. You're making me blush now, and men hate to do that. It's virtually impossible to blush and look tough at the same time—did you know that?"

She knew he was being silly to make her feel better, but unlocking his room with him in it? There wouldn't be any feeling better about that for a long time.

"Seriously, even though I would have liked to know before you went and got her, I'm glad you were there for her. That's what matters."

"I'm sorry I didn't wake you up. So now we're even. Let's forget it. Okay?"

She nodded. "Since my most embarrassing moment is officially ended with no hidden cameras or ten-thousand-dollar prizes, I have to get back downstairs to work."

He was kind enough to laugh at her feeble attempt at humor. "See you in about ten minutes for lunch. Sub sandwiches, right?"

"Yep." She started to leave then paused. "Quick question. Since you're here all the time, instead of just occasionally like most guests, are the menus too predictable for you?"

He ran his hand through his hair and regarded her solemnly. "Brandi, you have my word that absolutely *nothing* around here is too predictable."

Before she could form an answer in her shell-shocked brain, he grinned. "And I wouldn't have it any other way."

❧

"Jake? Got a minute?" Brandi asked from the doorway.

"Sure." He followed her into the den.

In the four days since she'd burst into his room, she'd definitely been avoiding him. The fact that she was seeking him out now piqued his curiosity and gave him a surprising surge of pleasure.

He occasionally took a two- or three-day break from training to speak to schools. His trip to Missouri had been scheduled for a long time, and if he hadn't left so irritated in the middle of the night he'd have told Brandi. But he never dreamed she would think he'd moved out. He grinned as he remembered how aghast she'd looked when she saw him sitting at his desk. And how pretty once the color came back to her face.

Brandi sat on the couch and motioned him to the chair catty-cornered from her. She opened her mouth then shrugged. A now-familiar pink stained her cheeks. "It's hard not to feel awkward around you, after I made such—"

He held up his hand. "Stop. It's forgotten. We agreed, remember?"

She smiled. "Okay. This is about Michael. Have you talked to him much lately?"

"Other than to tell him and Melissa I'd pay them ten bucks to wash my truck today? No." He frowned. "Should I have asked you first?"

"No!" She waved her hand dismissively. "Don't be silly." She looked toward the doorway and lowered her voice. "Michael wants me to sign a permission slip so he can play football."

"Well, is that a problem?"

"Not really. I think Dad and Mom will be okay with it, but—I'm not sure Michael has the right motivation."

How much motivation does a kid need for playing seventh-grade football?

When she frowned, he realized he'd said the words aloud. "I'm sorry. But I don't see the problem with signing his consent form unless you're worried about his getting hurt."

"Maybe you're right. But would you talk to him about it? See if you can draw him out a little bit. I guess what I'm saying is I'm not sure he really *wants* to do this." She twirled a strand of hair with one finger.

Jake stared at her. Her beauty was breathtaking, but the caring concern in her blue eyes, even though he knew it was for Michael, made his chest ache with an emotion he couldn't define. He cleared his throat. "I'm just heading out to check on the truck clean-up mission. I'll see what I can find out."

Relief erased the lines in her forehead. "Great. I really appreciate it."

Jake found himself looking for a way to prolong the conversation. "Hey, I'm supposed to meet Elizabeth and her husband, Steve, Friday night at the pizza parlor. Why don't you come with me? Elizabeth would be absolutely thrilled."

"Oh, I don't know. . . ." Brandi glanced down at her hands. "I'm going back to California when Mom and Dad get home. And you'll be hitting the road again as soon as your shoulder is better. We probably shouldn't. . . ." Her voice faded away.

"I like you, Brandi." He realized as he said the words how true they were. He did like her, but he also knew there was no future in it. "I don't need a relationship right now any more than you do. It wouldn't be a date. Just a bunch of old friends— and one new one for you, counting Steve—getting together for pizza."

Her face brightened. "That sounds like it would really be fun. If you're sure Elizabeth won't mind."

"I'm positive."

"Great." She stood and motioned toward the dining room. "I guess I need to go see how Valerie's getting along with her chores."

He nodded and stood. "I'd better check on my truck." He turned to go.

"Jake."

He glanced back. "Yes?"

"I'm glad you asked me to go."

His heart thudded against his ribs. Was that tenderness in her eyes for him this time? "I'm glad you said yes."

ten

Jake walked out to where the preteens were hard at work washing his truck.

"Hey, guys. How's it going?" He grabbed a brush and tackled the bug-crusted windshield.

"A lot better," Melissa assured him.

"Better?"

Michael snorted and waved his soapy sponge. "Yeah. Better since I let her have the water hose."

Jake grinned. He should have figured they'd both want to spray the water. He remembered arguing with his brothers over the same thing when he was young.

"Melissa, why don't you use it for ten more minutes then let Michael have it for a while?"

Melissa nodded.

"So, Michael, Brandi tells me you want to play football."

"Yes, sir."

Jake restrained a grin. The Delaney kids were a neat mixture of old-fashioned manners and modern savvy.

"He's just doing it so the kids will think he's cool," Melissa said, clutching the water hose with both hands and neatly shooting Michael's sponge off onto the ground.

"I am not—hey! Be careful." Michael scooped up the sponge and glared at his sister.

"You like football, Michael?" Jake asked, keeping his eyes on the window he was scrubbing.

The boy mumbled a reply.

"What?"

"I said not so much." He shrugged. "Okay, she's right." He narrowed his eyes at Melissa. "But at least I don't eat worms to be popular."

"Hey!" Melissa punctuated her exclamation with a blast of water in Michael's direction, but the stream fell about a foot short. "I was in kindergarten. Give me a break."

Jake didn't speak for a few minutes. Surely no one could live very long and think God didn't have a sense of humor. How was Jake supposed to advise a boy about participating in a sport in order to feel good about himself? When he'd figured out he had a natural talent for baseball, he'd mostly worked hard to pursue it because he wanted to find his own place among his bigger-than-life brothers. By the time he outgrew that motivation he had other, more complicated, ones.

"Going out for a sport is a big commitment." Jake took Michael's sponge and directed him to a new section of the truck. "You won't be able to miss a game or practice, even when you're working hard on a new invention. Are you sure you're willing to be there for every practice, every game, day in and day out?"

"I'm pretty sure." The twelve-year-old scrubbed furiously, but his face clouded with indecision. "I don't know."

"Mike, buddy. You've got an incredible amount of talent and intelligence." Jake cleared his throat. Michael was looking up at him as if his words were a lifeline for a drowning man. Melissa had let the water hose aim at the ground and was listening intently, too. "Most important, you have a Father in heaven who made you just the way you are and loves you that way. And so do your family and friends." He squeezed the boy's shoulder. "So, whatever you decide about football, you don't need sports to prove you're somebody. God's already done that for you."

The kids worked in silence for a while. Jake didn't know if it was because they were considering what he'd said or if he'd embarrassed them with his lecture. He felt like a hypocrite telling Michael not to play football unless he loved it. But then again comparing seventh grade and the majors was like comparing a 1972 compact sedan to a 1965 sports convertible.

A stream of water droplets slid down the windshield, hit his brush, and veered off, zig-zagging toward the hood. Jake could sympathize. It seemed as if he'd suddenly been deflected willy-nilly onto an uncharted path. He had no idea where he was going.

Three weeks ago he'd had plans. Goals. Direction.

Now he knew only one thing for certain. If he didn't manage to chase these doubts away, his career truly was as kaput as all the sports writers said it was. Coming back from a bad injury was tricky enough. Many tried and failed. It was all in having the tenacity to see it through.

He knew some of his confusion was caused by the blond he'd fished out of the water. That was nothing new. She'd had the same effect on him when he first met her eight years ago. Even though she wasn't quite as prickly now, she distracted him from his goal. And distractions were something he couldn't afford.

He tossed the brush in the bucket. "I've got to walk over to Coach Carter's. Think you guys can handle this?"

"Sure." Melissa said.

"We can if she'll let me use the sprayer." Michael held out his sponge to his sister.

She made a face but handed over the water hose. As Jake walked away he heard her say, "See, Michael? I told you, you didn't need to play football."

❧

"You've got a date with Jake?" Valerie squealed.

"No, we're just meeting some friends for pizza."

"Like I said—a date. Are you nervous?"

"Well, I wasn't." Brandi grimaced. How could she explain to her sister that a nomad baseball player would be the last person she'd date? Valerie had been six when they moved in with Gram after Gramps died. She didn't remember the years before spent on the road, moving from place to place. Brandi would never forget the feeling of not belonging anywhere.

She pulled the front part of her hair back in a clip, leaving the back hanging down. One more glance in the mirror, and she spun around on the vanity stool to face her sister. "What do you think?"

"Why are you worried about it, if it's not a date?"

Brandi blew out an exasperated sigh and stood. "Just forget it. Do you think you can handle things tonight?"

"Hmm. I've been dealing with guests since I was ten. I'm pretty sure it won't be too much of a challenge."

"Great."

Valerie grinned. "You'll be home by midnight, right? We wouldn't want to change those rules Mom and Dad made oh-so-long-ago."

Brandi didn't want to encourage the sassy teen, but she couldn't bite back a chuckle. "Yes, smarty. I'm sure I'll be home long before midnight. No turning into a pumpkin for me."

"Actually that was the coach that turned into a pumpkin, not Cinderella."

Brandi suddenly remembered how literal Valerie had always been. So many things like that she'd forgotten since she'd moved back to California. Seeing someone twice a year didn't allow a lot of time for close bonding. It was strange. She didn't realize how much she'd missed her sisters and brother until she was with them again.

She hugged Valerie. Her sister resisted for an instant but then returned her embrace.

After a minute Valerie pulled back and peered up at her, brow furrowed. "What was that for?"

"Because I love you."

"Hmph. I love you, too. But if you ask me, you're just excited about your date."

Brandi groaned. "You'd better go get changed since you're in charge tonight."

Valerie nodded and slipped out the door. Brandi grabbed a light jacket from her armoire. Her sister leaned back into the room, an impish grin lighting up her face. "By the way, you look fantastic."

"Thanks, Val."

"Anytime," Valerie called over her shoulder as she bounded down the hallway.

Brandi shook her head. How could there be such a shifting mix of sunshine, rain, and fire in one person? Sometimes she worried about getting older, but she was immensely thankful not to be a teenager again.

❧

"I hope Elizabeth and her husband don't mind my tagging along," Brandi said, as she and Jake walked out to his truck.

"They'll be thrilled. Especially Elizabeth. I can't wait to see her face when she realizes who you are." Jake grinned. Elizabeth had always bemoaned the fact that she'd lost touch with Brandi.

"If you say so. I still think we should have called."

"You worry too much." Jake opened the moon roof then turned on a CD of classical music mixed with nature sounds. "Just relax."

She glanced at him, apprehension apparent in her eyes, even in the moonlight.

He smiled. "Don't worry. No ulterior motive here. Just one friend trying to help another to chill out."

"When you start playing Mozart and Beethoven accompanied by birds and thunder instead of Cotton-Eyed Joe, I'm thinking maybe it's time to worry."

He threw back his head and laughed. "I have very eclectic tastes in music, I'll have you know."

"Yeah, well, you've successfully hidden them until tonight." She flashed a white smile.

"Maybe we haven't given each other a chance until tonight." He wished the words back as soon as he'd said them.

Her smile disappeared. "Look, Jake. I know we agreed this isn't a date. But there are some things you need to know if we're going to be friends."

"Like what?" He thought he could probably guess most of them, but he knew she needed to tell him.

"You know I didn't want to move here at the beginning of my senior year."

"Yes."

"That's probably an understatement. I detested the idea and did everything but chain myself to the mailbox."

He smiled at the image. "Sounds as if you were a lot like Valerie."

Her eyes widened, but she nodded. "I guess I was." She picked at imaginary lint on her pants. "Anyway, I begged my parents to let me stay with Gram, but they decided a 'simpler life' was better for all of us and insisted I come to Arkansas." She glanced at him, and pain flashed in her eyes. "You know how well that worked out. All of you hated me. And I have to admit the feeling was mutual."

Jake started to protest, but she held up her hand. He guided the truck into the pizza parlor parking lot.

"I promised myself that when I got back to California I would control my own life. And except for a few things not worth mentioning"—another flash of pain—"I have. If I have a flat, I fix it. If there's a spider in my closet, I kill it. But invariably people, especially men, think I need 'taking care of.' " Her face reddened as if she regretted saying so much. "They're mistaken."

Jake stared at the most independent woman he'd ever met. "You seem perfectly capable of taking care of yourself to me." He closed the moon roof and turned off the stereo. "I'm sorry if I've ever made you feel otherwise."

A strand of hair had come loose from her clip. He wanted to brush it back, but he was afraid if he did, the tenuous connection they'd forged would break.

"Let's go eat some pizza," he said.

"I can't wait. It's made fresh daily, you know."

He laughed. He could remember her making fun of that sign eight years ago.

But she was all grown up now. As if to prove it she tucked her hair neatly back in place with no help from him.

❧

When they walked into the pizza place, Brandi felt as if she were stepping back in time. Right inside the door a crowd of people stood waiting to be seated. Jake nudged her, but she'd already spotted Elizabeth's long red curls. Jake made a "shh" motion with his finger and stepped in front of Brandi. He tapped Elizabeth on the shoulder.

She turned around, and her face lit up. "Jake! It's great to see you." Elizabeth had replaced her soda-bottle lens glasses with contacts. Her green eyes danced. The tall man beside her smiled warmly and walked forward to embrace Jake.

Brandi noticed he had a slight limp. Elizabeth hadn't changed a bit since high school. She'd always looked out for the underdog.

"I have a surprise for you," Jake said.

Brandi almost laughed at the excitement in his voice. He

was like a kid at Christmas.

He stepped over. "Remember Brandi Delaney?"

Elizabeth squealed and grabbed Brandi in a hug. "It's so great to see you! I can't believe it." She stepped back and held Brandi at arm's length then hugged her again.

Brandi smiled at her old friend. Her exuberance was contagious. "It's wonderful to see you, too."

Elizabeth introduced her husband to Brandi; then for the first time her smile faltered. "I have a surprise, too."

She reached for a young woman about their age who'd been standing next to Elizabeth, studying a menu on the wall. Grabbing her by the arm, she pulled her over. "This is Denise Simms, our new librarian. Since Denise hasn't been in town long, I thought it would be good for her to get to know some people." Elizabeth's smile was back in full force. "So now she gets to meet two people instead of only one. This is wonderful."

Denise looked like someone had just driven a Rototiller through her begonias. She seemed to be speechless.

Panic washed over Brandi like a wave. She'd stumbled right smack into the middle of a surprise blind date for Jake.

eleven

Brandi's face grew hot. She knew they should have called.

"It's nice to meet you, Denise," Jake said, shaking her hand. His smile was so genuine there was no doubt he meant it.

Brandi nodded. "Yes, it is."

"Y'all, too," Denise half-whispered. Her brown hair was swept elegantly into a French twist, and her makeup was flawless. She'd obviously put a lot of effort into tonight.

Brandi considered excusing herself and calling Gram to come get her, but she decided that would make everyone even more uncomfortable than they already were.

As they stood in line for a table, Jake kept the conversation going so smoothly that Brandi couldn't help but be impressed. He had never been a country bumpkin, but he was pure class tonight. He drew each one out in turn. By the time they were ushered to their table—a round table for six rather than the booth Elizabeth had first requested—it was almost conceivable she had truly planned this gathering as a get-acquainted pizza party instead of a blind date. Until it came time to sit down.

Brandi decided to hang back and take whatever seat remained vacant. Apparently so did everyone else. So they ended up doing the pizza parlor version of a Mexican hat dance until Elizabeth finally pushed Steve toward a chair and said, "Sit!" She plopped down beside him. For the first time since the whole awkward night began, a flash of uncertainty crossed Jake's face.

Brandi yanked the chair out next to Elizabeth and sat

down. A moment later Jake pulled out the chair two seats down from her, and Denise slid in with a gracious thank-you. Then he sat between them.

Brandi couldn't imagine that the first round of a major-league baseball draft could have been any more difficult or required more finesse than this seating ritual.

"So, Jake," Elizabeth asked. "How's your shoulder?"

"It's a little better. I have a reevaluation week after next with the team docs. But I'm pretty much resigned to the fact that I'll be out the rest of this season."

"Will they let you do any pitching warm-ups at all?" Steve asked.

Jake shook his head. "Nope. I'm hoping they will after this check-up, but for now just cardio training."

Brandi stared at them. She'd been living in the same house with Jake for almost four weeks, and she'd learned more about his life in the past two minutes than she had in all that time. She needed to take a serious look at her people skills.

"You travel a lot, don't you?" Denise asked, looking up at Jake, eyes shining. What Brandi had mistaken for a half-whisper earlier was really a sultry alto voice.

"Yes." Even though his face was turned partly away from her, Brandi could see him responding to Denise's warm smile with one of his own. "I travel with the team during the season, and then I travel regularly, speaking, during off-season."

"Your program to discourage drug abuse among teenagers, right?" Denise touched Jake's arm. "I think that's fascinating."

For the next ten minutes all eyes were on Denise, who kept up a running stream of questions for Jake. She only stopped when the harried waitress finally came by to get their drink order. Brandi had a sinking feeling it was going to be a long night.

What had this girl done? Read a short biography of Jake

McFadden in preparation for this evening?

"How did you get involved in your teen drug and alcohol prevention program?" Denise asked, as soon as the waitress left.

Jake hesitated a minute. "When I was in college, one of my buddies on the team was injured in an alcohol-related accident." He stopped as if considering what else to say.

"So, Brandi," Steve broke in. "Your parents said you're in computer programming."

"That's right." Was it her imagination, or had her voice grown rusty from non-use? Maybe she was subconsciously mimicking Denise's tone. The come-hither voice sure seemed to hold Jake's attention.

Brandi cringed at the catty thought. This was an uncomfortable situation for everyone, and it wasn't as if she and Jake were really on a date. She'd been listening to Valerie too much.

"And you have a software company?"

"Yes, we do." He looked fondly at Elizabeth. "Even though the software Elizabeth uses most is a word-processing program, we're partners in the business."

"I know." Brandi touched Elizabeth's arm. "Jake told me you were a best-selling author. I can't wait to read your books."

"They're absolutely delightful," Denise piped in. "Have you read them, Jake?"

"Yes, I have. Elizabeth has a real way with words." Jake tore his attention from Denise and smiled across Brandi at Elizabeth. Brandi was just glad to see his head could still swivel both ways.

"And so do you." Denise placed her hand on Jake's arm, bringing his gaze back to her. "I've read your journal on your Web site. You have such a heart for teens."

Brandi felt her blood pressure rise. The librarian was like a perpetual wind-up doll.

"Oh, you've read my journal?" Jake asked. "My Webmaster insisted I add that. I told him no one would read it." He chuckled. "I'll have to call him and let him know I was wrong."

"You sure will. I have an e-mail reminder sent to my inbox every time there's an update," Denise said.

Can anyone say stalker? Brandi thought irritably then shamed herself again. She knew there was no future for her and Jake, so why was she letting Denise's obvious attraction to him bother her? Especially since Jake seemed to be eating it up.

The waitress appeared with their drinks and took their pizza order. Denise squealed with delight when she and Jake ordered the same thing. Brandi couldn't help but wonder if his favorite pizza had been in his Web site journal. Resisting the urge to ditto their orders just to take the wind out of Denise's sails, she stuck by her veggie pizza preference.

"Jake, my man!"

Brandi groaned. That voice hadn't changed much in eight years. She looked up at Les as he pumped Jake's hand. He was still muscular and fit. He'd cut his blond curls into a buzz cut that gave him a more tough-guy look than he'd sported in high school.

Elizabeth's smile grew wider. "Les, why don't you eat with us? We ordered plenty."

"Ah. . . ." Les ducked his head, and Brandi thought the big guy might be blushing, but with his naturally rosy cheeks she couldn't be sure. "I just came in to order a pizza to take home. I'm not really dressed for it—" He motioned down at his uniform with its monogrammed name patch.

"C'mon, Les—stay. Girls love a guy in a uniform," Jake teased.

"You should know, McFadden," Les shot back. "That's the reason you play ball, isn't it?"

"Yep. That's the only way I can get them to notice me." Jake's good-natured grin amazed Brandi. His career hung by a thread, and getting it back obviously meant everything to him. How could he joke about it?

Les slid into the chair between Denise and Steve.

"Hi, Brandi, good to see you again," Les smiled at her across the table.

"Les, how are you doing?" Brandi asked.

"Pretty good." He looked at the librarian. "Hi, Denise. You look nice tonight."

"Hi, Les. Thanks." Denise's smile seemed more real than anything about her since they'd sat down. "We missed you Wednesday night."

This time Les definitely blushed. "I had a late tow call and couldn't make it."

Denise looked back at the rest of them. "When I first joined the singles' class at our church, Les was the only one who spoke to me. I think the others were a little intimidated by me."

Brandi quickly turned a snort into a cough.

The pizza arrived, and either because her mouth was full or because of Les's arrival, Denise finally wound down. By the time they had finished eating, Brandi had decided the woman wasn't as bad as she'd thought. With Les, the librarian seemed like a real person instead of an obsessed fan. Brandi's feelings were reinforced when the muscular blond offered to take Denise home and she accepted.

After they left, Elizabeth sighed. "That went well."

They all stared at her then simultaneously burst out laughing.

"What?" Elizabeth asked. "I prayed it would work out, and it did."

"You've still got it, Elizabeth. I don't know what it is

exactly, but you've still got it," Brandi said, squeezing her friend's hand.

"Denise isn't always so—talkative. I think she was probably nervous," Elizabeth said. "In case you couldn't tell, she's a big baseball fan."

Brandi nodded, feeling like an idiot for reacting the way a jealous girlfriend would.

"I'm so glad you came with Jake tonight. I'm just sorry I had other"—Elizabeth cleared her throat—"plans."

"Speaking of Denise," Jake said, drawing his brows together, "did I miss the part where you asked me if I wanted a blind date?"

Elizabeth put her hand to her mouth and giggled.

Steve shook his head, but love for his irrepressible wife gleamed in his eyes. "I warned her. But she wouldn't listen. Some nonsense about wanting everyone to be as happy as we are." He took Elizabeth's hand across the table and twined his fingers with hers.

Brandi thought she saw a flash of pain across Jake's face.

"Besides, we didn't know you were already going to have a date," Elizabeth added.

"It's not a date," Brandi said.

At the same moment Jake said, "We're just friends."

Elizabeth put up her hands. "Okay, okay. I get the picture."

But from the twinkle in the redhead's eye Brandi sincerely doubted she did.

ॐ

As they retraced their route back to the B&B, Jake glanced at Brandi. She'd been quiet ever since they'd said good-bye to Elizabeth and Steve outside the pizza parlor. "You okay?"

"Yeah, I'm fine." She twisted her mouth thoughtfully.

"Denise had a lot to say, didn't she?" In spite of the awkwardness of the evening Brandi had acted like the consummate lady. Not very many women would have handled the situation with such aplomb.

"Yes. Sometimes I forget you're a celebrity and people act differently around you from how they normally would."

Jake pulled the truck into the B&B parking lot and grinned at her. "So I'm just a regular joe to you, huh?"

"Pretty much." She tucked a strand of hair behind her ear.

"That's too bad. You're kind of special to me." He held his breath. That sentence came with a money-back guarantee to get her guard up.

A smile flitted across her face in the moonlight. "Jake—"

"I know. We aren't going there."

"You got it."

"Well, the night didn't turn out the way I thought it would." He knew changing the subject was his only hope of keeping her with him awhile longer. "I'm sorry for not calling Elizabeth ahead of time as you suggested." He grinned. "On the other hand, it sort of served her right to have to deal with the awkward situation she created, considering she set that up without asking me."

"What would you have said if she'd asked?" Brandi's casual question hung in the air.

"Why do you want to know?" Jake shot back.

Brandi shrugged and opened the truck door. "Just making conversation." She climbed out and slammed the door behind her.

Yeah, right. Miss California cared a little more about his social life than she was willing to admit. For some reason that realization warmed the loneliest corners of his heart.

He jumped out and jogged a few feet to catch up with her. As they walked up to the porch he wondered if she could hear his heart beating. Even though he knew it was too soon—who was he kidding? Even though he knew it should never happen, all he could think about was kissing Brandi good night.

He glanced over at her, blond hair streaming down her back like a silver curtain woven with moonbeams. When they stepped up to the door, he paused. She stopped and looked up at him. "I had a great time tonight, Jake. Thanks for asking me."

"Thanks for going. I had fun, too."

He leaned toward her, unable to read the expression in her sparkling eyes.

The front door opened. Valeric stood there with her hands on her hips. "I thought y'all were never coming home. Melissa's been in the bathroom hurling for half an hour."

Jake followed Brandi into the house. He tried to tell himself the interruption was a good thing, but his heart refused to believe it.

twelve

Brandi tossed the empty spray can of disinfectant into the laundry-room trash and pushed her hair back from her forehead. Dare she hope the ordeal was over? Melissa, Michael, and Valerie had each been sick with a forty-eight-hour virus, staggered out over the past four days. Brandi had isolated them all in Michael's large room on the first floor to keep them away from the paying guests.

The last thing they needed was word-of-mouth advertising for the sickest little B&B west of the Mississippi. Gram and Jake had escaped unscathed, and so far Brandi had, too, which was amazing considering she'd slept on a cot in the sickroom for four nights. Even though she was dog-tired, her stomach didn't hurt, and for that she was extremely thankful.

One good thing about the virus epidemic was that it kept her mind off the "almost kiss." For the most part. She'd still managed to relive the minute several times. Each time she tried to guess what she would have done if Valerie hadn't opened the door.

Her reaction usually depended on whether she had her eyes closed or open when she recreated the moment. In broad daylight she always pulled away and made some witty remark. But when her eyes were closed, she leaned toward him and surrendered to the sweetness of his kiss.

"What are you staring at?"

Brandi jumped. She was standing in the middle of the laundry room clutching a bag of dirty clothes.

Valerie stood in the doorway, eyebrow raised. "Talk about

104

zoned out! You've missed way too much sleep."

"You didn't complain when I was holding your head night before last." Brandi stuffed the sheets in the washer and poured in the detergent. The last four days and nights had been a dizzying spin of holding heads and doling out soda and crackers. Gram had wanted to help, but Brandi knew bending over would be hard on her back.

Valerie looked up from where she was sorting clothes. "You did good, sis. It was almost like having Mom home."

Brandi basked in her sister's praise. She'd worried the kids would think her a poor substitute. "I'm glad I was here."

"Yeah, me, too." Her sister kept sorting the laundry into piles, but she cleared her throat. "Brandi?"

"Yeah?"

"Did you ever have friends who completely changed?"

Brandi considered her question. "What do you mean?"

"Oh, you know."

No, I have no idea, but I'm trying. She sent up a silent prayer for help. *If I could still speak teenager-ese, maybe I could decipher this.*

"How did they change?" Maybe her casual tone would work.

"Well, they've always been just like me. We like boys, and we like to have fun, but we're different from a lot of the girls. Only this year they're not." Valerie glanced at Brandi and then back to the pile of whites. "You know?"

Think. Like boys, like fun. Different from a lot of girls; only this year, not. What did that mean?

Brandi felt like a rookie lion tamer. *How exactly do you not let them smell your fear?*

"So you're saying. . ." Maybe letting her voice drift off would make Valerie want to fill in the implied blanks.

"Yeah, that now they're just like everyone else, and they want me to be, too."

"Angie and Brit?"

"Well, duh. Yeah."

Okay, so far, so good.

"In other words they want to go to parties in Rainey's clearing and things like that." Brandi kept the casual tone in her voice.

Valerie nodded. "And if I don't, they won't be my friends anymore. And neither will anyone else."

"That's a rough choice, isn't it?" Brandi swallowed hard. She was way over her head here.

"That's what I'm saying." Valerie had dropped all pretense of working. "So what would you do?"

"Val, there's not an easy answer to that."

"No kidding. I made all A's last year. I figured if there was one, I'd know it by now."

Brandi had a hard time imagining her sharp-tongued sister giving in to peer pressure, but then she remembered another sharp-tongued senior whose life had been made miserable by a group of girls.

Anger coursed through her hard and fast at the thought of Valerie dealing with that. She suddenly related more to the mama lion than the lion tamer. "Thanksgiving isn't too far away. The school year is almost half over. I know this is hard for you to imagine now, but you'll be graduating right away. You know what you believe. It's not worth compromising that to make everyone like you, is it?"

"No."

"Is there anybody else you can be friends with until then?"

"Well, there's Jeannie. She's kind of cool, and we get along—but she's always got her nose stuck in a book." Valerie looked uncertain.

"Hey, I had a friend exactly like that in high school. Elizabeth Battlestone. Her name's Elizabeth Campbell now, and she's a best-selling author."

"Elizabeth Campbell was your friend?" Valerie's eyes widened. "*The* Elizabeth Campbell?"

Brandi nodded.

"You are so lucky! She came to school and spoke in assembly. I've read all her books. Wow!" Valerie shook her head. "You think Jeannie might end up like that?"

"You never know."

"It's worth a shot, huh?" Valerie asked.

Before Brandi could go into not making friends based on ulterior motives, Valerie laughed.

The dinner bell rang, and Valerie dropped the clothes in her hand. "Do you think we're germ-free enough to eat with everyone else now?"

Brandi nodded. "Let's go. Jake's the only guest here right now, anyway."

"Oh, well, who cares if we make him sick, right?" Valerie teased.

"I haven't seen him in four days. I'm pretty sure *he* cares," Brandi said. *Either that or he's staying away from me on general principle after the other night. Which would be smart.*

They washed their hands and walked into the dining room together. Melissa and Michael were sitting at the table on either side of Gram. Both kids got up and hugged Brandi even though they'd seen her that morning. Through their illness and forced isolation together, the Delaney siblings had turned a corner in their relationship with their oldest sister. In spite of her exhaustion Brandi couldn't help but be happy at the thought.

Jake hurried into the room and claimed the last empty chair. After he'd said the blessing for the food, he looked up with a smile. "So how are the sickos?"

"I think we're all well," Brandi said.

"Just when it's safe to breathe the air again, I have to leave." Regret tinged his words, and his gaze settled on Brandi like a warm blanket. She suddenly knew without a doubt he hadn't forgotten where they'd left off on the porch the other night.

"Leave?" Brandi concentrated on buttering her roll and tried to sound casual in spite of her pounding heart.

"Yeah, I'm heading to St. Louis to take in a few home games and see the team doc."

"Wow! Will you get to sit in the dugout?" Michael asked, bouncing in his chair.

"Of course he will." Melissa punched Michael on the arm. "He's part of the team."

"Melissa, don't hit your brother. Oh, Jake, I hope you get the news you're looking for," Gram said, without taking a breath between sentences.

Jake chuckled. "Thanks, Elva. I appreciate it."

Brandi passed Jake the green beans and, for a minute, considered the possibility of bad news concerning his shoulder. He wouldn't be on the road all the time anymore. He'd told her once that he'd managed to get a physical education degree in three years of college. Now there was a settled job. And they always needed coaches in California.

Shame pierced her heart. How could she be so selfish as to hope that his dreams were ground into dust just because they didn't coincide with hers? At the sound of Jake's voice she pulled herself back to reality.

"I didn't want you to worry I was moving out without letting the management know." His dimples flashed. "I'll be back in a few days."

Brandi took a sip of her tea. When had this man gotten under her skin so badly that the thought of him leaving for a few days made her feel empty? What would it be like when he was actually gone for good?

❧

Propped up against pillows, Brandi pulled another tissue from the box on her bedside table. She always cried when she watched *The Wizard of Oz*. How many times when she was little had she stood outside one rental house or another and clicked her heels together over and over, repeating, "There's no place like home"?

Too many to count. With each click she'd kept her eyes squeezed tight and focused on an image of the place she spent summers—her grandparents' place in Southern California. But every time she'd opened her eyes, she was still in front of whatever cheap little cracker box they were living in right then.

The credits rolled, and Brandi hummed "Somewhere Over the Rainbow" as she aimed the remote at the TV and flipped the channel button. An achingly familiar face stopped her finger in mid-push.

"Cardinals' fans welcomed Jake McFadden back to Busch Stadium this week, but unfortunately only as a spectator." The still photo above the anchor's shoulder changed to a tape of Jake smiling and signing autographs as hoards of fans gathered around him. Women reached for him as if he were Elvis.

The announcer's voice-over continued. "McFadden has attended several games this week, but he is in town for a re-evaluation of shoulder surgery complications that have kept him benched most of this season. Will he be back in the starting lineup soon, or is his career over? No one knows for sure, but this is what he had to say."

The camera zoomed to a close-up of Jake at an apparent press conference. He flashed his dimples and blushed at the complimentary remarks being yelled by the crowd, then spoke. "The doctors saw significant improvement in my shoulder. They're very pleased with the results of my cardio training.

I don't know about y'all, but those sound like positive results to me."

The crowd went wild, cheering and clapping until he held up his hand. "Lord willing, I'll be back on the mound very soon."

When the camera panned the audience, tears sprang to Brandi's eyes. Hundreds of people held up signs saying things like, COME BACK SOON! and WE MISS YOU, JAKE. More than one said, WE'RE PRAYING FOR YOU, JAKE.

The camera cut back to Jake, and his eyes were glistening. He cleared his throat. "Thank you all for your support. A special message before I go, for all you teens out there. Remember—if a friend offers you drugs"—he paused, but the audience finished for him, their voices booming as one—"he is NOT your friend!"

No wonder he was determined not to lose his career. She recalled snippets of conversation about his speaking program. He was on a mission as surely as her parents were. And he'd obviously do anything to stay in that particular ball game.

ॐ

Jake carried his suitcase up the sidewalk. It seemed as if he'd been gone forever. Would Brandi be downstairs when he came in? Had she missed him as much as he'd missed her?

He opened the door. "Brandi?"

"In here," she called from the den.

He left his suitcase in the foyer and walked into the den. She had the reservation book in front of her, and concern creased her forehead as she studied it. "Oh, hi, Jake," she said.

So much for his wondering if she'd missed him. Apparently she hadn't even noticed he was gone. "What's wrong?"

"Not much. I was looking at the schedule for the rest of October. We're going to be pretty busy. But we have a week off for Thanksgiving." She motioned toward the big calendar.

He nodded. At least she wasn't ignoring him. He walked over to look at the calendar. Was it his imagination, or did she stiffen? He didn't touch her, but he was close enough to smell the faint scent of her shampoo.

She turned suddenly, her blue eyes wide. Time seemed to stand still as he reached for a strand of hair that had come loose from her ponytail. He gently tucked it behind her ear and smiled. "I missed you, Brandi."

She took two steps backward and offered him a bright smile that didn't quite reach her eyes. "We missed you, too." She walked toward the dining room. "And I promise I didn't break into your room this time," she called over her shoulder.

Then she was gone, leaving him feeling as lonely as he had in St. Louis.

thirteen

"Surely there's somewhere we could go. A hot little spot where we could check out the night life around here and get to know each other better." The dark-haired man flashed a brilliantly white smile and looked around the empty den. "Everyone else is in bed. No one will even realize we're gone."

Brandi shook her head. About twice a month she got propositions from guests. Usually overconfident businessmen who thought she was wasting away here in the middle of nowhere pining for some male companionship. Mr. Fisher was no exception. "Thanks, anyway. I'm not much on the night life. But don't let me stop you." She bit back the urge to give him directions into town to the little all-night diner/donut shop the local police frequented.

"No, it won't be any fun by myself. C'mon, Brandi," he pleaded and reached for her hand.

She jerked away, thankful the reception table was between them. Up to now her lack of interest had always been met with disappointed acceptance. This man was a little more persistent. Maybe he needed her to spell it out. "Mr. Fisher, I'm not interested."

"Well, maybe you shouldn't smile so pretty at everyone if you're not interested." An ugly sneer replaced the puppy-dog pleading look so quickly Brandi almost gasped aloud. He started around the table.

"I—" Brandi weighed her options. She could scream. Or—her hand closed over a paperweight on the desk. She could hit him.

"I believe the lady asked you to leave."

Brandi stared at Jake looming in the doorway. Was it her imagination, or had her hero just stepped out of one of the black-and-white movies she loved so much?

"She didn't mean it. She wanted—"

Jake strode into the room and towered over the businessman. "I'll tell you what. You've got five minutes to pack and vacate the premises. Starting right"—he looked at his watch—"now!"

The dark-haired man gaped, and so did Brandi. Jake *had* stepped right off the screen of an all-night, movie-channel, classic hero extravaganza. Except he was real.

Fisher apparently decided he was real, too, because he bolted for the stairs.

Jake turned to Brandi. "You okay?"

"I am now. Thanks." He didn't have to know her legs felt like noodles. "You seem to make a habit of rescuing me."

"I hope you didn't mind my asking him to leave. You can add his room charge to my bill."

"I don't think that'll be necessary." She held up the paperweight. "I'm sure it's cheaper for the B&B to have a vacant room than it would have been to pay for stitches to Mr. Fisher's head."

Jake laughed. "You had it under control, didn't you?"

"Possibly, but your way of handling it was much more fun. I felt like I was watching an old John Wayne movie."

"Oh, no. You're not going to start calling me Big Jake?"

She raised an eyebrow. "I was thinking more along the lines of one of his lesser-known movies—*Angel and the Badman*."

"Yeah, right."

Bumping sounds echoed into the room from the staircase. "Sounds like our 'pilgrim' is packed and ready to go," Jake drawled.

Mr. Fisher appeared in the doorway and tossed the key on the reception desk. "Thanks for nothing."

"You, too," she called as he slammed the door.

She showed the key name tag to Jake. "Guess what room he was in?"

Jake leaned forward to read the lettering and laughed. "GONE WITH THE WIND. How fitting."

He stayed beside her as she put the key in the box.

"Well, that little encounter got my adrenaline pumping." Either that or her pounding heart was due to the fact that Jake was just inches from her, looking at her as if he wanted to swoop her into his arms.

"Sounds like you need to wind down." He grinned. "At the risk of sounding like Fisher, would you like to go for a walk?"

More than anything. "I guess I'd better not. Thanks, though."

Jake nodded, disappointment clouding his eyes. "Oh, well, at least you didn't hit me with a paperweight." His chuckle sounded forced.

She offered a weak smile. "I wouldn't dream of it."

He shifted awkwardly. "Good night then. Sleep well."

She bit her lip against the urge to pour out her heart to him. To explain that she too felt the connection but that she was protecting them both by not allowing their relationship to grow. Instead she said, "Good night, Jake. Thanks again," and stared at the rug until he left the room, so he wouldn't see her tears.

❧

Jake jogged over to where Coach Carter held a stopwatch. He ran in place while the older man read the display.

"Your cardio fitness is better than it was when you first got benched, boy."

"Thanks to your pushing." Sweat ran down Jake's face in spite of the terrycloth band he wore on his forehead.

Coach snorted. "Thanks to your determination. I've never seen anybody more anxious to get back into something they were already a little tired of."

Jake shook his head. "Sure, I told you the lifestyle gets old after awhile. But, as I've also said, I want to stay in because I see the impact I can have on kids' lives, helping them stay off drugs." He grinned. "And if I can get a 'God loves you' in every once in a while, I like that even better."

Coach Carter nodded. "I understand. But you have your coaching degree. Have you ever thought about having a huge impact on a few instead of a little impact on many?"

"Sure. I've thought about it." Jake nodded. "But do you realize how many kids I influence?"

"Are you sure it hasn't stopped being about God and started being about you?" Coach asked.

Jake frowned. "I'm positive." If anyone else had asked him that, he'd have hit the roof, but Coach had known him his whole life. "You always said you'd tell me if I got 'too big for my britches.' Is that what you're trying to tell me?"

"Not at all." Coach pulled off his Cardinals cap, smoothed his gray hair back with his hand then screwed the cap back down on his head. "Here's what I'm gettin' at, Jake. Is this speaking program God's will for you, or is it your will for you? Does that make sense?"

Jake massaged his tight shoulder. "Yeah, it makes sense. I guess we'll find out when I go back to the doctor in a couple of months. If it's not healed by the end of December, then it's over."

"So do they think it will be?"

"Yes, actually it's improved a lot. Right before I left, Doc Watson told me we could add in some pitching warm-ups. He thinks I'll be back on the field by spring training."

"I guess you're excited then."

Jake didn't speak for a few seconds. Except for the one night he'd taken care of the obnoxious guest for her, Brandi had barely spoken to Jake in the month since he returned from St. Louis. He should be excited about the prospect of playing again; but he had a sinking feeling that when he did, Brandi would become so distant as to be invisible in his life. "I don't want to get my hopes up." He punched his coach on the shoulder. "Elva tells me you two have been seeing each other. Is it serious?"

To Jake's surprise Coach Carter blushed. In all his years of knowing the man he had never seen him blush.

"It could be." Coach cleared his throat. "It *will* be if I have my say."

"That's wonderful! Does this mean you'll be moving to California?"

"I would, in a heartbeat, if Elva wanted me to."

Jake understood that all too well. Brandi had the same effect on him, but he couldn't afford to allow it to keep him from his goal—the goal he knew God had given him. Regardless of what Coach thought.

&

"Look, Brandi! No cane!" Gram called as she walked up the sidewalk.

Brandi glanced up from the porch planter she was filling with bright yellow mums. She tossed her trowel down and jumped to her feet, wiping her hands on her jeans. "Gram, that's fantastic! Look at you go!"

When the older woman reached the porch, Brandi pulled her into a hug. "How are you feeling?"

"I still have some pain, but I think I'm getting there. Dr. Barnes says I should be as good as new by Christmas." Gram's eyes sparkled. "And I'm praying he's right."

"Me, too."

"Actually, Thanksgiving would be nice. Guess what?" Gram sat in a rocker and motioned Brandi to one.

"What?" Brandi sat beside her with a quizzical grin. More than a missing cane was exciting Gram. Her whole face glowed. "Tell me!"

"Ben has asked me to his sister's for Thanksgiving."

Brandi leaned forward. "Really? Are you that serious?" She knew they'd been dating some, but she had no idea they were ready to meet each other's families.

Gram took Brandi's hand. "I don't know. But I've never really wanted to date since your grandfather died. Ben's just"—her smile grew wider—"different. When I'm not with him, I feel incomplete." She squeezed Brandi's hand. "And life's too short to feel incomplete."

Brandi thought of all the sappy black-and-white movies she'd watched during Jake's long trip to St. Louis last month. Even his occasional two-day trips were almost unbearable. Yet when he was around, she refused to allow personal conversation, instead holding him at arm's length. Gram was right. Jesus had even said He had come so people might have life and have it more abundantly. But He hadn't said anything about coming so they might hoard it like emotional misers.

"Penny for your thoughts."

Brandi jerked her head up to see Gram, brows knitted together.

"Child, you looked like you were a million miles away."

"I was just thinking about what you said." She patted Gram's hand. "I'm so happy for you and Ben."

Jake's truck pulled into the driveway.

Brandi gave her grandmother a speculative look. "Gram, do you think you're up to handling things tonight?" She nodded toward the house. "Valerie's friend, Jeannie, is sleeping over, or I'd ask her."

"I'll be glad to take care of everything, honey. Are you going out?"

Brandi eyed Jake who had started up the sidewalk. "I might be."

Gram laughed. "Tired of feeling incomplete?"

"Exactly."

"In that case I think I'm going to go check on supper." Gram pushed to her feet and dropped a kiss on Brandi's cheek. "I'm proud of you."

"Thanks. I'm proud of you, too."

Gram slipped into the house as Jake reached the porch.

"Did I run her off?"

"Not exactly." Brandi grinned at him. "I think she might have thought we needed some privacy."

Jake spiked an eyebrow. "Privacy? Why?"

"I'm not sure, but she may have thought you'd be embarrassed if I asked you out in front of her." Brandi felt her face grow hot, and she grimaced. "Or maybe she thought I would be."

He shook his head. "Now I'm confused. You want to run that by me again?"

"I need to get out for a while. I thought you might like a rain check on your invitation from the night Mr. Fisher got out of hand."

"You want to go for a walk?" Jake asked.

She almost laughed at the confusion in his eyes. Poor guy. He probably thought she was crazy.

"A walk would be fine. Or dinner and a movie. Whichever you prefer."

A grin spread across his face. "Dinner and a movie sounds great!" He looked down at his jogging shorts and T-shirt then at his watch. "Obviously I need a shower. Would seven be okay?"

"Hey! Who's doing the asking here, mister?" Laughter bubbled up in her throat. "But, yes, now that you mention it, seven will be fine." Gram was right. Life was too short to waste.

fourteen

Jake relaxed in the easy laughter of the blond across the table. The barbed-wire fences and insurmountable walls Brandi had built between them for the last month were gone. As a matter of fact, the Brandi who wouldn't even look him in the eye had vanished.

In her place sat the warm, caring woman he'd seen glimpses of now and then—the woman he so desperately wanted to know better. And that woman, either by design or by accident, was rapidly entangling his heart with hers. He prayed it wasn't an accident.

"So what made you decide to—" He weighed his words, unwilling to say the wrong thing and risk reconstructing the wall.

"Ask you out?" She grinned, mischief glinting in her eyes.

"Yep." He leaned forward and covered her hand with his. When she didn't pull back, he gently caressed her skin with his thumb. Did she feel those sparks?

She stared at their joined hands for a few seconds. When she looked up, he saw a hint of fear in her eyes. So she *had* felt it.

ൠ

"I decided I haven't been very fair to you. Or to me. We deserve a chance to see what happens without worrying about California or being on the road. Life's too short to be so practical." Her voice held a quaver that hadn't been there a minute before. "Unless I've totally misread you and you don't want a chance to see what happens?" She pulled her hand from

120

under his and tucked a loose strand of hair behind her ear.

"No! I do." He felt like a teenager, tripping over his feet to assure her he was interested.

"It feels weird to be away from the B&B, doesn't it?" She ran her finger along the edge of her plate.

"You should get out more often." He took a drink of tea.

"So should you."

"The B&B feels like a little bit of heaven to me. I get my fill of 'out' when I'm on the road." Jake cringed and tossed his napkin on the table. If they ever discovered a way to take words back, he hoped he was on the list of first to be notified.

Her face clouded. "I don't see how you live like that. Especially since you travel all winter, too, with your speaking schedule." She took a sip of her tea and regarded him intently over the rim of the glass.

He shrugged. "It's not as bad as you think." He felt his ears grow hot as he tried to put his thoughts into words without bragging. "Um. . .money makes travel a lot more palatable." He lived modestly for his income, but the idea of her comparing the transient life of an itinerant worker to the comfortable traveling he did was ridiculous.

"Physically I guess it might." She offered a twisted smile. "But it would still be awful. No place to call home."

"Most all the guys have a permanent home. They're not on the road during the winter."

"Do you have a house?" Brandi asked.

"No, but I travel so much in the off-season for my work with teens, it's been easier for me to find lodging on the road. I stay with my parents some or one of my brothers when I'm at loose ends."

"Don't you want to have your own place?" Puzzlement creased her brow.

"Sure. I'm getting ready to. I've looked at some places around here. But the B&B fits my needs for now."

"Would you care for dessert?" Their waitress motioned to the tray laden down with a variety of pastries and cakes. She balanced it in one hand.

"Brandi?" Jake asked, and she shook her head.

"No, thanks."

"Me either, but thanks." Jake smiled at the tired woman.

"Say, aren't you—you're Jake McFadden!"

"Yes, ma'am."

She plopped the tray down on the table and pulled out her order pad and pen. "May I please have your autograph for my son? He's thirteen, and he talks about you all the time." She stopped and eyeballed his arm. "How's your shoulder?"

When he saw Brandi cover a grin with her napkin, Jake ran his hand down over his eyes and rubbed his chin with his thumb, giving her a mock-threatening look. He smiled at the waitress. "It's better. Thanks." He held the pen over the paper and looked at the waitress's name tag. "Louise, what's your son's name?"

"Leroy."

He scrawled a quick note to Leroy then flipped the paper over and wrote one to Louise.

After the waitress left, calling to her friends in the kitchen, he raised an eyebrow at Brandi. "You thought that was funny, did you?"

She pulled the napkin down, a grin tugging at her lips. "I just keep forgetting you're a celebrity."

"You've said that before." He struck a Johnny Bravo pose. "Maybe this will help."

She collapsed into giggles. "That does NOT help."

"Oh. Well, then maybe it's better you forget."

"I have to admit it's easier when you're just Jake who lives in CASABLANCA." Her giggles faded to a bittersweet smile.

"In that case, here's lookin' at you, kid."

She groaned but laughed again as he hoped she would. As long as he kept her mind off his career, maybe he had a chance with her. Unfortunately, come spring training that task might prove impossible.

⁊

"Do you want any more popcorn?" Jake held the almost empty container over the lobby trash can.

She shook her head. "No, thanks. Now you know why I didn't eat dessert. I was saving room for movie junk food."

He dropped it in the trash, and they headed for the doors, along with the departing crowd.

"So what did you think about the movie?"

"I loved it. Did you?" She glanced up at him as they were jostled along to the exit.

He held the door open for her to step outside. "Yes. Action, adventure, romance, and a happy ending. What's not to like?" As the crisp autumn breeze swept across the parking lot, he clasped her hand in his and guided her toward the truck.

She shivered.

"You cold?"

"A little." A very little, but what was she supposed to say? *The electricity surging up my arm when you took my hand made me shiver?*

He shrugged out of his denim jacket and wrapped it around her shoulders. As soon as they started walking again, he reclaimed her hand.

"Won't you get cold?" She clutched the coat around her with her free hand and breathed in the smell of his aftershave.

He lifted their connected hands. "Not as long as I'm holding on to you."

"Now there's a macho line if I've ever heard one."

"Maybe so, but true." He opened the truck door for her and waited until she was in.

As he walked around to get in, she thought about how easy their camaraderie had been tonight. She'd been dragged kicking and screaming into this relationship. Not by Jake, but by her own fascination with this good-hearted, funny, compassionate man. And on the porch this afternoon, after she talked to Gram, she'd let go. She'd released her grip on common sense and caution and gone along for the ride, willingly and with her eyes wide open.

She glanced at him as he started the motor. His shoulder seemed to gain strength every day. He'd soon be leaving. And in spite of Gram's "life is too short" speech, Brandi knew his departure would hurt worse now than it would have before. But for tonight it was worth the future pain.

"You okay?"

She forced a smile. "Yes." Suddenly she longed to have some questions answered about the past. So she wouldn't spend another eight years wondering.

"Remember that night you took me to Dana's party?"

Jake looked over at her. "Sure."

"Did you ask me out just to make Tammy jealous?"

Jake jerked his gaze toward her. "No way. I asked you out because I'd wanted to all year. Once Tammy and I broke up, there was no reason not to."

Relief flooded her at the lie exposed even after all these years. He had been a nice guy then, too.

"Well, after Stephanie spilled soda on my blouse—"

"Wait a minute. I thought you spilled it yourself."

Brandi turned to look at him. "Why would you think that?"

"Because Tammy said you told her in the bathroom that you'd dumped soda on yourself to get out of the rest of our date."

"Oh, Jake." Brandi chuckled sadly. "We fell for her line, didn't we?"

"Hook, line, and sinker." Jake shook his head.

They rode in silence until Jake pulled into the B&B and parked.

She reached for the door handle, but his voice stopped her.

"Brandi?"

She looked back at him.

"Would it be okay if we say good night here? I'd rather not take a chance someone might be waiting by the front door to yank it open." His dimples flashed.

She knew what he was asking. Someday when she was left with a heart full of regrets and "what ifs," this one would have been much easier to handle if he'd just kissed her, instead of asking permission. Nevertheless she nodded.

He took her hand and drew her close. She stared up at him in the moonlight. His eyes, alight with wonder, caressed her face. He outlined her jawline with his thumb. This time when she shivered, he wrapped his arms around her and touched his lips to hers. All the worries of the future fled like leaves in the autumn wind.

He pulled back and looked at her again, a million questions in his eyes. Whatever he saw in her answering gaze seemed to freeze the words on his lips. "We'd better go in," he said hoarsely.

She blew out a soft sigh of relief and regret then nodded. "I think you're right."

fifteen

"What do you want, Brandi? Do you want the moon?" Jake's whisper echoed George Bailey's words next to her ear. Brandi nudged him, but she couldn't stifle a grin. She'd been thrilled when he'd decided to join them for a family movie on one of their rare scheduled "empty nest" nights, as Valerie called them. Gram was out with Ben, and Jake's presence graced the atmosphere with a homier feel. Of course there was also the fact that she loved being around him.

"Shh. . ." Melissa twisted around to glare at the couple on the couch then turned her attention back to the screen. "This is a great part."

Valerie reached out with her toe toward her sister. "You 'Shh,' squirt. You're being louder than they are." She was curled up in the chair closest to the TV.

"And you're being louder than she was," Michael complained from where he was stretched next to Melissa on the floor.

"Look what I started," Jake said quietly.

Brandi shook her head with a mock frown. "You'd better be quiet, or you'll get in trouble. *It's a Wonderful Life* is pretty important around here. I cheated by getting it out before Thanksgiving."

He took her hand, and she shivered.

"Are you going to do that every time I touch your hand for the rest of our lives?" he whispered very softly.

She didn't answer, but her cheeks burned. *The rest of our lives?* A tiny shard of pain sliced through her happiness.

Could she throw away her long-sought security for this man?

They watched the movie in silence. When the credits rolled, Brandi slipped her hand away. She didn't want to explain about Jake to the kids. Mostly because she didn't have a clue what to say.

Melissa pushed the power button on the remote and stopped the tape. "I know it's sappy, but I love that movie. I'm glad you didn't make us wait until Thanksgiving."

Brandi grinned at her sister. She'd noticed Melissa moping around lately. Even though the kids spoke to their parents on the phone twice a week, with the holidays approaching, their absence was wearing on the ten-year-old.

"Speaking of Thanksgiving," Jake said. "I have an invitation for y'all to come to my brother's house and have dinner with my family."

"Will any kids be there?" Melissa asked, scrambling to her feet.

"Almost more than I can count."

"Can we?"

Brandi looked at Melissa's pleading face then at Michael, who nodded.

"Didn't you say you had a nephew who's eighteen?" Valerie asked.

"Yep."

She looked at Brandi. "Sounds cool."

Brandi didn't think meeting Jake's family was the best idea with so much undecided between them. But how could she say no to three kids who were going to spend Thanksgiving an ocean away from their parents?

"Is it at Senator McFadden's house?" Brandi knew from Gram that the state senator and his wife lived about fifteen minutes away. Close enough to jump in her car and come back to the B&B if she was uncomfortable.

"Yes, but you can call him Holt and his wife Megan. They would love to have you all."

Brandi nodded. "Okay. Thanks. If you'll give me her phone number, I'll call her to see what I should bring."

Jake beamed. "Great!"

"We're going!" Melissa skipped around the room.

"Right now the only place you're going is to bed," Brandi said.

The two preteens chased each other through the foyer.

Valerie rolled her eyes. "They've got empty-nest syndrome," she explained to Jake. "When we don't have overnight guests, they go wild."

Jake chuckled.

Valerie stood up. "I guess I'm going to turn in. Unless you two need a chaperone."

Brandi raised her eyebrow. "I think we're fine." She got up and hugged Valerie. "Nice one, Val," she whispered in her ear. "I'll get you back someday."

Valerie winked at her and headed for the stairs. "Don't stay up too late," she called over her shoulder.

They heard her shoes slapping every step.

"I don't think Michael and Melissa are the only ones with empty-nest syndrome," Brandi said, grinning. "She's a mess."

Jake nodded. "But a nice mess. And she seems to be doing a lot better."

"Yep. I thank God for that every day."

"Guess what I thank God for every day?" Jake asked and pulled her back down beside him on the couch.

Brandi gulped. He was thanking God for her? "Jake, maybe we should talk."

He put his finger to her lips. "Shh. If it's the moon you want, I'll lasso it for you, you know."

She grimaced. "Something far more complicated than that,

I'm afraid." She ran her fingers through her hair.

"Brandi, we could buy a house anywhere you want to live. California or New York. Both. I don't care. And you could go on the road with me as much or as little as you wanted. Then when I could get away—"

Tears filled her eyes. He was unwittingly spelling out her worst nightmare. "Jake, can we put this conversation on hold? I know that's asking a lot, but with Thanksgiving coming up, I'm just not up to talking about this."

"Sure." He dropped a kiss on her forehead and stood. "Cookies and milk?"

"Now that's an offer I can't refuse." She smiled, but she followed him to the kitchen with a heavy heart.

❧

A tap on the door pulled Brandi's attention from her Bible reading. "Come in."

Gram walked in with a cup of coffee in her hand.

"Gram! You're upstairs again." She took the coffee and kissed her grandmother's cheek. "Thanks."

"I was hoping we could talk for a minute."

"Sure. Sit down." Brandi indicated the two chairs in the corner. When Gram chose one, Brandi sank into the other. "What's on your mind?"

"I'm not going back to California."

Brandi tried to draw a deep breath, but she felt like a vise had squeezed her chest. "You're not?"

"I'm sorry, baby." Gram's voice trembled. "I knew this would be hard for you to understand. But I've been with you all these years, and now it's time for me to be close to the other grandkids for a while."

"And Ben?" Brandi hated the flatness in her voice. She tried out a smile, but she was sure it probably looked as painful as it felt.

Gram nodded. "Yes, and Ben. Who knows where this will go? I sure don't, but as we talked about before, life is too short not to take chances."

"I understand."

"I'm going to go ahead and give you my house."

Tears filled Brandi's eyes. She'd always known Gram planned to leave her the house, but that was supposed to be years down the road—when the unthinkable happened.

"It's the only real home you've ever known, and I realize how much it means to you."

Brandi nodded and swiped at her tears with her hand.

"Unless you don't want it?" Gram raised her eyebrow, and Brandi knew she was thinking of Jake.

"No, I do. Thank you so much, Gram. It's my home, and I love it." Brandi couldn't believe it. Her house was actually *her* house now.

The older woman patted Brandi's knee. "Honey, I hope you'll remember that a house is just mortar and bricks. It takes more than living somewhere a long time to make a home."

Brandi sniffled. *Tell that to the perpetual new kid in school.*

"And if you ever decide you don't want it, I don't have any qualms about your selling it. My memories aren't in those walls. They're in here." She tapped her chest.

Brandi hugged her grandmother close. "I love you, Gram."

"I love you, too, honey. And I'm praying for you every day."

Jake's words about thanking God for her every day flashed through her mind. "Thanks. Are you able to take over the B&B again if I need a substitute?"

"Definitely, but I'm sure hoping you'll stay through Christmas. Why?" Concern knitted the older woman's brow. "Is it your job? Have they called you back early?"

Brandi shook her head. "No, nothing like that. But I

wanted to know what my options were."

"It's always nice to have options, isn't it?" Gram asked, smiling gently.

Brandi snatched a tissue and stood. "I can't believe you're staying here."

"Honey, sometimes you have to follow your heart. You'll do the same thing one day."

Brandi shook her head. "What if your heart goes in two different directions?"

Gram chuckled. "You always did ask the hardest questions." She stood. "I think you'll have to figure that one out for yourself."

"Thanks a lot."

"You'll do fine." Gram enfolded her in her arms. "I'm proud of the woman you've grown into, Brandi."

The older woman slipped out the door, leaving a trail of honeysuckle in her wake. Brandi wondered how long it would be before the house in California lost that precious scent.

❧

"Son, come in." Jake's dad opened the door and ushered his son inside. "Everything all right?"

Jake nodded and accepted his dad's proffered hand. As always it progressed into a hug. "Yeah, sorry. I should have called. I was just hoping to talk to you for a little bit."

"Elaine! Come see who's here!" His dad ushered Jake into the living room.

"How's your shoulder?"

"It's better."

"I'm glad."

Jake wondered what his dad would think if he couldn't go back to baseball. It would no doubt be a disappointment.

"Jeb, did you call me?" Jake's mom stepped into the room, and her face split into a big grin. "Jake! Where did you come from?" She ran to hug him.

He kept his arm around her shoulder and turned back to his dad. "You're the luckiest man I know. She gets younger-looking every day."

"You've been kissing the blarney stone again, I see," his mom chided.

His ears burned. Did kissing a Delaney girl count? He was pretty sure she was of Irish descent.

"Cat got your tongue?" she asked, with a rueful grin.

"Nope. I stand by what I said. No blarney involved."

"Oh, honey, you're so sweet." She stretched to kiss him on the cheek. "Come on in and sit down."

She motioned him to the chair next to his dad's then perched on the couch. "Is everything okay?"

"I've already grilled him," his dad said.

"Oh? Are we having him for supper?"

Jake's dad gave his mom a hard look. "Very funny, Elaine."

She turned to Jake with a grin. "He thinks he's the only one with a sense of humor." She stood and patted his arm. "I'm going to let y'all talk while I go whip us up something to eat. You'll stay for supper, won't you?"

"I thought you'd never ask."

She hurried to the kitchen.

"She's really excited you're here. We don't see you often enough, Jake."

"I know. It's hard for me to get away between training and speaking at schools. I'll definitely be at Holt's for Thanksgiving." He considered telling his mom and dad about Brandi, but he didn't want to jump the gun. Anything could happen between now and then.

"Holt said you'd know for sure in late December whether you'd be signing a new contract with the Cardinals."

"Yep." Jake instinctively massaged his shoulder. "I'm doing a lot better though, so I have a good feeling about my chances."

"That's what you want then?"

"Yeah, I think so."

His dad pinned him with a look that had always made him confess that, yes, he had done whatever it was in question. "You *think* so?"

Jake nodded. "If they offer me a new contract, I'll sign."

His dad looked as if he wanted to say more, but he just nodded. "I'll be cheering for you whatever you decide."

sixteen

"We could have all fit into Jake's truck, you know." Valerie balanced Brandi's pecan pies on her lap and nodded toward the crew-cab truck leading the way. "And the toolbox had room for all the food."

"I know, but Jake has Michael and Melissa with him and their skateboards and bicycles." She rolled her eyes. "Which I still can't believe they talked him into taking. Anyway, I prefer to have my own car." Valerie's argument was old hat, since Jake had come into the kitchen that morning saying the same thing.

Brandi didn't know how to explain that when she was going to meet a huge group of strangers she preferred to have her car in case she needed to make a quick getaway. So she'd just shrugged then. She did it again now.

"You really need to work on your control issues, sis." Valerie gave her a cheeky grin. "You have a good thing going with Jake. Don't blow it."

"When are you hanging out your shingle, Dr. Valerie? Or are you just going to start with your own call-in radio show?"

"Very funny. Did you know people use sarcastic humor to deflect attention from their problems?"

"Really? Is that why you do it? Maybe we should talk further about what makes you tick." Brandi looked at her watch. "But, oops. Speaking of tick, our time is up for this week." She raised an eyebrow at her sister, silently telling her not to dish it out if she couldn't take it.

Valerie held up her hands then quickly grabbed the bobbling

pecan pies on her lap. "Okay, okay, I give up."

"You let those pies fall, and I'll show you 'give up.' " Brandi's grin belied the gruff words.

"I wouldn't dream of dropping these. I'm too impressed you actually baked them from scratch. Not that I think I'm the one you were trying to impress."

Brandi blinked against a sudden flash of insight. If she didn't live so far away, she and Valerie could be close friends. Their sense of humor was actually very similar.

"Hey, where's your comeback?" Valerie asked.

"I was just letting you bask in your wittiness."

Jake put on his blinker, so Brandi followed his truck down a partially wooded lane. Up ahead she could see a huge two-story white house with a green tin roof. It looked elegantly old-fashioned and yet meticulously cared for.

"Wow!" Valerie breathed.

Brandi was nodding her head in agreement, until she caught the direction of Valerie's gaze. A well-muscled teen with dark hair was throwing a football to a group of younger boys scattered out over the rolling hills of green grass that surrounded the house.

"Yep. And the house is pretty impressive, too," Brandi muttered.

Once they were closer to the house and out of eye-range of the junior Ricky Martin, Valerie grinned at Brandi. "Guess what, sis? It's time to play Meet the Parents."

Jake parked the truck and motioned to Brandi to pull in beside him. When she rolled to a stop, he came to open her door. "Is it okay if the kids go on and play and I help you carry the food in?"

Brandi nodded.

"Valerie?" Jake leaned in the car. "Do you want to take Michael and Melissa and introduce them to the other kids?"

"Um. . .sure." Valerie's saucy demeanor disappeared. She looked as nervous as Brandi felt.

Brandi turned to take the pecan pies. "Val, it'll be fine. Just be yourself."

Valerie nodded and climbed out of the car. Michael and Melissa joined her, and the three youngest Delaneys went to meet the McFaddens. Brandi watched them go with trepidation. Now she had to face the rest of the clan alone. No sooner had the thought formed than Jake took one of the pies in his left hand and clasped her free hand with his right.

"We'll come back and get the rest of the food after we say hello." He didn't loosen his grip on her as they walked up to the enormous porch. She glanced at their entangled hands. Was he being nice? Or was he afraid that if he let her go she'd kick off her shoes and run for the hills?

"This is the house I grew up in."

"Really? I love it!" She could picture Jake as a child playing hide-and-seek with his brothers here. The thought made her smile. "Where do your parents live now?"

"Lakehaven. We've always had a vacation house there, but they moved into it permanently a couple of years ago, and Holt and Megan bought this place."

Brandi thought of Gram's house. Her house now. Did Holt treasure living in the house he'd grown up in as much as she did?

"But Holt's going to sell it after the first of the year. They want a smaller place closer to Mom and Dad and Megan's folks."

Brandi cringed. What about all the memories?

The question quickly fled from her mind as they stepped onto the porch. Her stomach clenched. "What if they don't like me?" she whispered to Jake as they approached the door.

"We don't deal in impossibilities. They'll love you."

The front door opened before Brandi could change her mind and hightail it out of there.

"Jake! It's so good to see you." A petite woman with fine blond hair clasped Jake in a one-armed hug. She smiled at Brandi. "I'm Megan, Holt's wife. You must be Brandi."

"Nice to meet you," Brandi murmured and returned Megan's warm handclasp. "I know you said not to bring anything, but I made a couple of pecan pies and a few other things. I hope that was okay." Jake had told her that, in spite of Megan's polite refusal, food was always welcome at a McFadden family gathering. She hoped he was right.

Megan took both pies and breathed in deeply. "Mmm. . . pecan. My favorite."

"Mine, too." A red-haired woman had appeared behind Megan and deftly snagged a pie from her hand. She grinned at Brandi and extended her empty hand. "I'm Jessa."

"I'm Brandi." They shook hands, and Jessa looped her arm with Brandi's.

"I'm so glad you came. Let's go get acquainted."

Megan latched onto her other arm, and Jake excused himself to go get the rest of the food from the truck. What had that death grip on her hand out on the sidewalk been about? He'd given up easily enough when faced with two of his sisters-in-law.

For the next hour she tried desperately to match names with faces. Jessa was so much like Brandi's friend Elizabeth that it was easy to feel she knew her. But the others blended together no matter how hard she tried to keep them separate.

"I know exactly how you feel."

She turned to see a smiling woman with long brunette hair. The fireman and the florist. No, that was Clint and Jessa. This was Cade's wife. The boys' ranch. "Annalisa, right?"

"Yes. You should have seen me the first time I met Cade's

whole family." Her smile sparkled in her eyes, and Brandi liked her immediately. "There weren't any sisters-in-law, but with all the other relatives to remember I was a nervous wreck. It took me forever to get everyone straight. You're way ahead of me."

Brandi smiled. "Not really. I'm just playing word association games and winging it."

Annalisa held up her hand and laughed. "I don't even *want* to know what you're associating me with." She motioned toward the desserts that dotted the counter. "Can you help me with these? Megan has a special table set up for them out on the porch."

"Sure." Brandi grabbed a big flat tray that had apparently been laid out for that purpose and filled it with pies and cakes.

"And don't worry about the names. A year from now you'll wonder how you ever thought they were confusing."

Warmth rushed to Brandi's face. "I—"

Annalisa waved her hand in a don't-worry-about-it motion. "I know. You think you won't be around in a year." The brunette seemed to read her mind. "We all thought the same thing when we first met the family. But you just wait and see."

Brandi swallowed her protest. This sweet, funny woman didn't need to hear it. She'd see for herself at the next gathering when Brandi was absent. The thought cast a shadow over the sunny day.

❧

Third down, ten yards to go. The kids huddled around Jake and Holt, listening for the coming play. Jake grinned when Melissa sent a furtive glance toward Cade and Clint's team. "Psst, Melissa. Pay attention to our plan. Don't worry about them."

She turned back to him. "Okay, but they've got Juan and

Valerie. It's a wonder we've even managed a tie. We mostly have little kids."

Protests broke out among the teenage boys, and Jake raised the football over his head. "Listen up!"

When he had their attention, Jake looked over at the other team as if seeing them for the first time in spite of the fact that the game was almost over. "They do have bigger players, don't they, Holt?"

Holt nodded.

"But we've got"—Jake lowered his voice to a whisper, and all the kids leaned in automatically—"a secret weapon."

"What is it?" they chorused.

"Shh!" Holt put his finger to his lips. Jake almost laughed aloud as his brother gave him a puzzled look over the heads of the kids. "Tell them what our secret weapon is, Jake."

"Sarah." Jake whispered her name.

Sarah's blue eyes widened as everyone looked at her. "Me?"

"Yes, you. The key to winning a tag football game is to have an element of surprise. You're ours. Remember the other day when we were playing with the tennis ball?"

The eight-year-old nodded, her brow puckered.

"You caught it every time."

"Uncle Jake, that was a tennis ball." She leaned forward and looked up into his eyes. "This is a *foot*ball."

"You can do it. Just pretend it's small and round." He turned to the others. "Nobody will be expecting me to pass to Sarah, so here's what I want y'all to do. . . ." He spelled out the plan so everyone knew where to go.

"Ready?"

Just as Cade's twelve-year-old son, Tim, hiked the ball, Brandi walked up to the sideline with Jake's sisters-in-law. Jake glanced toward her and felt the ball hit him in the chest. Instinctively he grabbed it, but his eyes were still on Brandi.

Since the other team was watching Jake's eyes, their gazes all pivoted toward Brandi, too. Recovering his senses he tossed the ball to where Sarah stood near the opposite sideline. He held his breath as the ball fell into her arms and she clutched it to her. The little girl froze for a split second, as if she couldn't believe she'd really caught the ball, then ran for the water-hose goal line. The other team scrambled after her, but she crossed the line into the end zone before they got close.

"Touchdown! We won!" Everyone from both teams ran to hug Sarah and pat her on the back.

"Way to fake them out, Jake," Holt called above the din.

Jake nodded. Brandi looked up from where she and his sisters-in-law and his mom were talking. She winked. He suddenly realized the truth. Everyone else may have thought Jake staring at her when he caught the hike was part of his strategy, but she knew he'd truly been distracted by her presence.

"Good game." Cade clapped him on his good shoulder and followed his gaze to the group of women. "You've got it pretty bad, little bro. I've never seen anyone take your attention from a ball game."

Jake grinned. So he hadn't fooled everyone else after all. "Yeah, I can't believe I did that. I thought she was in the kitchen, and then she walked by. . . ."

"Can't think of anything but her, right?"

Jake shook his head. "It's not really that I can't think of anything but her, but she's there in everything I think about. Does that make sense?"

Cade nodded. "Perfectly. I was the same way with Annalisa." He grinned and looked at his wife a few yards away. "Still am, if you want to know the truth."

"But you and Annalisa—that was meant to be. Brandi and I are polar opposites. You two are like two peas in a pod."

Cade snorted. "Yeah, well, it wasn't always that way."

"Heads up!" The football landed on the ground between Jake and Cade.

Holt ran over to pick it up. "Sorry, guys. That was Clint's fault."

"Mighty nice of you to let me take the blame," Clint drawled. He walked up to his brothers. "I told him to go out for a pass. But I forgot he can't jump. So I take the blame for that."

"I can jump—" Holt started then shook his head and looked at Jake. "Hey, did your shoulder do okay in the game awhile ago?"

Jake gently took his shoulder through a range of motion. "Yeah, it did. No pain at all."

"That's great!" Clint patted him on the back. "I can't wait to see that no-hitter I know you're going to pitch next season."

"Thanks." Jake grinned at the thought. "Me, too."

"So, Jake," Holt said, winking at the others, "since your shoulder's better, I guess you'll be able to help us move by spring."

"There's a thing called spring training, you know. I'll be busy." He looked up at the big house and thought of the loads of furniture to be moved. "Very busy." He caught Brandi's gaze across the grass and winked. He couldn't be sure, but he thought she blushed. "I have to talk to Brandi." He walked away leaving his brothers arguing about who would help Holt move.

"Hey."

A bright smile lit her face. "Nice play."

"I couldn't have done it without you."

She wrinkled her nose. "All I did was walk by."

"And all I did was look." He took her hand. "But together we make a great team."

seventeen

"Brandi!" Elizabeth motioned from the little table in the corner.

"Hi—sorry I'm late."

"I called the cops thirty seconds ago," Elizabeth said with a quick glance at her watch. "You're a minute and a half late. You need to lighten up a little."

Brandi laughed. "And you've changed. How did you beat me here? I seem to recall having to rush you in between every class to keep you from being tardy."

Elizabeth grinned ruefully. "Steve's working at home today, and he pushed me out the door so I'd be on time."

Both women looked up as the waitress approached their table. "Do you both want the buffet?"

They nodded.

"Drinks?"

"Sweet tea," Elizabeth said.

"I'll have the same." Brandi sank back in her chair. "I'm glad you asked me to lunch, Elizabeth. Do we have an agenda? Or are we just catching up?"

Elizabeth chuckled. "You know me too well. We have a small agenda, but we're going to catch up, too."

Brandi raised her eyebrow. "Should I be worried?"

"Not at all. There's a winter carnival coming up at high school. Have the kids mentioned it?"

Brandi nodded. They'd all three brought notes home about it. She'd found Michael's crumpled up in the kitchen next to the cookie jar, Melissa had passed hers on happily, and Valerie had grunted when Brandi asked her if she had a note. "I don't remember much about it though."

"Well, let's fill our plates, and I'll tell you about it." She headed toward the food bar, and Brandi followed.

They grabbed plates and started with the salad bar.

"So, anyway," Elizabeth said, loading her plate down with salad, "the tenth, eleventh, and twelfth grades are doing this as a fund-raiser. The rest of the school and all of the community are invited to come. It's next Saturday."

"Okay, and you're giving me a personal invitation because—?" Brandi smiled as she took a liberal helping of salad dressing.

"Because I need your help. The eleventh grade has asked the Friends of the Library to help them set up a bookstore, and in exchange they're willing to give us twenty-five percent of their earnings."

"So you don't have enough Friends of the Library, and you need to bring in friends in general, huh?" Brandi teased.

"Something like that." Elizabeth wrinkled her nose. "Seriously, we have plenty of people to work the bookstore, but I was hoping you'd help me get it set up. I'm doing a book signing, too, so I'll have to fix a table for that as well."

"I'd love to."

"Great!" She honed in on the chicken tenders. "That was too easy. I'll finish my agenda when we get back to the table."

Brandi walked back to the table and waited for Elizabeth. They thanked God for the delicious food and then ate in silence for a few minutes.

"Now that I've given you a decent period of time to take the edge off your hunger, on to the second item." Elizabeth grinned.

"Shoot."

"Steve's company needs a good computer programmer. Since that's your area of expertise, we thought you might be interested in the position."

Brandi almost choked on a lettuce leaf. "Elizabeth," she rasped after she swallowed it, "I live in California."

"Well, I know that, silly!" Elizabeth said. "But people relocate all the time. Your family lives here, and I heard down at the diner that your grandmother is staying in town."

Brandi shook her head. The phrase "news travels fast" didn't do justice to this town. "Elizabeth, I really appreciate the offer. It means the world to me that you would trust me that much. But Gram is giving me her house. I'm going back in December. It's where I've lived since eighth grade." She grimaced. "Except the year I made everyone miserable around here."

"You didn't make me miserable. I've always thought you were an answer to my prayers. Before you came, Tammy and her group ran over me constantly, but you gave me the courage to stand up to her. I really appreciated it."

Brandi stared at her salad. She'd never dreamed that anything good had come from her year in Arkansas. "I'm glad."

"Well, we're not officially taking applications for the job until January, so if you change your mind. . . ."

Brandi touched Elizabeth's hand. "Don't save it for me, Elizabeth. I promise to keep in touch this time, but California is where I belong."

"I understand completely. It's been great seeing you again, and I'm going to hold you to your promise about keeping in touch."

Brandi gave her a mock frown. "Hey, I'm not leaving yet. I haven't even had dessert."

"Oh, good. Over dessert you can fill me in on the juicy details of your so-called friendship with Jake. What's this about Thanksgiving with his family?"

Brandi cocked a brow. "More diner rumors?"

"You betcha!" Elizabeth chuckled as she made her way to the dessert bar.

❧

Brandi left the kids outside talking to their friends whose parents or siblings had come early to help set up the winter carnival. She gasped when she walked into the gym. The bleachers had been retracted, and the whole area was decorated with artificial snow and spruce trees. A faux ice-skating pond with cardboard skaters formed a focal point in the middle of the building. Busy workers were adding last-minute details while Christmas music blared from speakers along the walls.

The book fair dominated one corner, complete with red and green balloons. Across the gym Elizabeth looked up from spreading a bright red cloth over a rectangular table and waved. She pointed toward the huge sign that announced "HOMETOWN AUTHOR ELIZABETH CAMPBELL" with an exaggerated Vanna White move. Brandi made a clapping movement then laughed when Elizabeth took a bow.

"You two haven't changed a bit since high school," Jake said in Brandi's ear.

She jumped. "Where'd you come from?"

"If the eleventh grade is going to win with me at the helm, I figured I'd better come check out our setup."

He gestured toward the carnival booths lining the far wall of the big building. Everything from balloon darts to a milk-bottle toss conspired to entice both children and adults to part with their money. Brandi spied a booth with a sign hanging in front of it: JAKE MCFADDEN AUTOGRAPHS—$1.00.

She bit her lip against a grin. Jake motioned to her to look up. She burst out laughing. The huge banner over the carnival booths boasted a caricature of Jake's face. Dimples as deep as the Grand Canyon framed his bright smile, and a diamond-like twinkle sparkled from his blue eyes. The words next to the picture proclaimed JAKE MCFADDEN GAME GALLERY.

"Wow! You're all that and a bag of chips, aren't you?" Brandi said when she could talk without laughing.

"I'm not sure they still say that anymore." Jake picked up a beanbag and tossed it at her.

"Who cares?" She caught it and threw it at the milk bottles. "We know what it means." She looked up again at the banner and shook her head. "Was this your idea?"

"No, actually I wanted them to put something up there about my campaign against teen drug use." He held up his finger. "And don't even look at me like that. I'm kidding!" He glanced back at the flashy gigantic poster. "But it wouldn't have hurt if they'd have at least mentioned it."

"Maybe next year."

"Yeah, maybe so." Jake strolled alongside Brandi as she walked over to help Elizabeth.

"Hi, Jake, Brandi." Elizabeth took a second to grin at them before going back to her book arranging.

Everything looked ready to go. "Um, Elizabeth. What am I supposed to do?"

"Oh. Well, I didn't expect to have so many people helping with the bookstore, and I figured I'd have to do that. But since they came to set it up, it only took a minute to get this ready."

"What are the seniors having?" Jake nodded toward an elaborate arrangement of curtains and folding chairs.

"A fashion show," Brandi answered. "I remember Valerie mentioning it." She frowned. "Not much seems to be going on there."

"Well, that's actually what I was getting ready to ask you." Elizabeth straightened the pile of books she'd just arranged. "The person who was supposed to do that didn't show up. They were wondering if you would fill in."

"Me?" Brandi squeaked. "Why would 'they,' whoever they are, think of me?"

"Maybe because I told them you'd be wonderful at it."

"What do I have to do?"

"Just oversee the seniors and describe the fashions as the girls come out."

"As in over the loud speaker?"

Elizabeth nodded.

"C'mon, Brandi. You'll do fine," Jake said.

"Easy for you to say. Why don't I sign autographs and let one of you two do this?"

"I knew you'd do it. Thanks so much." Elizabeth jumped up and ran off to tell the powers-that-be that she'd coerced Brandi into running a fashion show of all things.

"Did you hear me say I'd do it?" she asked Jake.

"In so many words."

Brandi shook her head.

Twenty minutes later she was holding on to a podium and announcing the girls wearing their home-economics fashions. At least she had note cards. All eyes were on her as she waited for the next model to come out when she felt someone tap her on the shoulder.

"Hi, sweetie." Tammy Roland's smile didn't reach her eyes, but it was beautiful enough that most people wouldn't care or notice. She slid the microphone from Brandi's hand. "I'll take it from here." She held her hand over the mic. "What's your name again? Ginny?"

"Brandi Delaney. Jake's girlfriend." Elizabeth had suddenly appeared at Brandi's side. "Nice of you to finally show up, Tammy."

Brandi, head held high, walked to the back of the seating area, trying to ignore her burning cheeks.

Tammy's sultry laughter filled the gym. "Let's give a big hand to Brandi Delancey, who was a good sport to take a stab at emceeing in my absence."

The audience politely applauded. When Brandi knew they weren't looking at her anymore, she turned to Elizabeth. "Why didn't you tell me she was coming?" she hissed.

"She's been on again, off again, more times than I can count. And when she didn't show by ten minutes till, I didn't think she was going to put in an appearance."

"She's here now. Bigger than life. You could have warned me she was a possibility."

"I'm sorry, Bran. I knew if I did you wouldn't have come."

"You've got that right," Brandi muttered and looked over to where Jake was still in his booth signing autographs for an exclusively male line. That and the game booths gave the men something to do during the fashion show. Had he known Tammy was coming?

"So was that why you really wanted me to come, Elizabeth? Because you knew Tammy would be here?"

Elizabeth shrugged. "Look—she's always been able to get her claws back into Jake. I didn't want that to happen again. He's crazy about you. I thought if you were here, the contrast between the two of you would make his choice clear."

Brandi's heart sank. Elizabeth obviously thought Tammy could have Jake back in a second if she wanted him. "I understand. Listen—I think I'm going back to the house. I'll come pick up the kids when it's over."

Elizabeth grabbed her arm. "Since when do you let Tammy Roland control your actions?"

Brandi shook her head. "Nice try, but I'm still going."

She walked outside and breathed in the cold air. Her face still burned from Tammy's attempt to humiliate her. Since she'd left her jacket under Elizabeth's table, maybe the embarrassment would keep her warm.

"Brandi."

She spun around to see Jake running down the sidewalk. "Wait."

"What's up?" She tried for casual.

"I missed you."

"Shouldn't you be in there signing autographs?"

He reached for her. She let him fold her into his jacket. "Everybody deserves a break."

The steady beat of his heart soothed her raw nerves. She didn't know how long they stood there on the sidewalk. Only that she heard a snatch of a Christmas carol as the door opened and someone yelled, "McFadden, we need you!"

He pulled back and tilted her face up toward him with his finger. "Please come back in. I don't want to be away from you a minute tonight." Something she couldn't define lurked in the shadowy depths of his eyes. Regret?

She nodded and allowed him to take her hand and lead her inside.

⁂

Jake took a sip of his soda and looked across the gym. Brandi and Michael were throwing darts at balloons and laughing. What would happen when he went to St. Louis? His shoulder didn't hurt at all anymore, and he felt positive they'd offer him a new contract. No way could he turn it down.

The noise of the carnival swirled around him, but he let it go for a minute.

God, thank You for all the blessings You've poured down on me. We both know how unworthy I am. I need Your help again. In my small understanding this door seems to be locked, but I know there's a window somewhere for me to crawl through. You've always given me one when I've gotten in a tight spot, but this time I'm not seeing it. Help me convince Brandi that traveling doesn't mean she has to give up her family or having a home. Or prepare me to live without her. In Jesus' name, amen.

❧

"Brandi, how nice to see you again."

Brandi took her soda from the lady at the concession stand and turned slowly. She knew that voice. "Tammy."

The girl hadn't changed a bit, from the Southern drawl to the perfectly made-up face.

"So you're Jake's off-season romance." Tammy put a manicured hand on Brandi's arm.

Her venomous tongue hadn't changed a bit either. Brandi's hand ached with the desire to spill her soda accidentally on the model's white pantsuit. "I have to go." She slid her arm from the other girl's grasp.

"Wait." Tammy's eyes narrowed. "Just a word of advice from someone who knows. You may think he loves you, but when he gets out on that field it's all about him and being in the spotlight." The brunette smiled sweetly and started to walk away.

"Tammy."

"Yes?" Tammy turned back and arched one perfectly plucked eyebrow.

"Why do you hate me so much?" She honestly didn't want to have it out with Tammy, but she'd always wanted to know.

"Hate you?"

Oh, here it comes. Little 'ol me? Hate you? What are you talking about, honey child?

Instead Tammy leaned in close and spoke in a low voice. "You came in with your California tan and your long blond hair and tried to take what I'd worked for years to get. I sent you packing then. But I won't have to this time. If you want to travel around and play second-fiddle to a little white ball and hoards of screaming fans, then you're welcome to him until he gets tired of you." Somewhere in the numb disbelief inside Brandi's brain, the fact registered that Tammy had lost her accent. "Has he told you why he plays baseball?" Tammy chuckled. "I see he hasn't. Ask him about his friend who was bound for major-league ball but ended up in a wheelchair instead because of your precious Jake. Guilt has Jake so twisted up he has to be some kind of a saint instead of a real man." She threw her hair back over her shoulder. "If I'd have been satisfied with that, I'd still be with him. So how special does that make you?"

Before Brandi could reply, Tammy was regally threading her way through the throng of kids.

"Brandi? Are you okay?" Concern covered Melissa's face.

"Yeah, honey, I'm going to be fine." Brandi put her arm around her sister. "I think it's time to go home, though."

eighteen

Jake let himself into the house and stepped quietly into the foyer. He'd felt as if he had to stay and help clean up, even though his mind had been on Brandi's abrupt departure. And, since all the nightlights were on, it looked as if she'd already gone to bed.

"Hi." Brandi's voice floated to him from the den. He peeked in the doorway, and she was sitting in the semidarkness on the couch, knees up, clutching a throw pillow.

"Hey, there. You feeling okay?"

"I guess."

He sat down beside her on the couch. "What happened back there? Why did you leave so quickly?"

Brandi shook her head. "I'd had all of Tammy I could take."

Jake's heart sank. Tammy. He should have known. He'd managed to avoid her, but it hadn't been easy. "What did she say?"

Brandi looked up at him. "A lot of things. None of them good."

"You know how she is, Brandi. How she did us in high school."

Brandi rested her chin on the throw pillow. "Yeah, I know."

"So are you going to tell me what she said that upset you the most?"

"Are you playing ball because of what happened to your first baseman when you were in college?"

Jake frowned. He'd intended to tell her the whole story, but it had never been a good time to disillusion her about him.

"What did she tell you?"

"That you had a buddy who was headed toward the major league but ended up in a wheelchair because of something you did. So you've been trying ever since to live out his dream for him."

His mouth twisted into a distorted grin. "Well, for once in her life Tammy told the truth."

"Jake, what happened?" Brandi put her hand on his arm. In spite of the fact that she was obviously upset by her confrontation with Tammy, concern for him tinged her voice.

He put his head back against the couch and stared up at the soft yellow glow of the nightlight on the ceiling. *Lord, please help her not to hate me.*

"Like I said that night when we had our blind date with Denise—he was in an alcohol-related accident. The rest of the story is that I was driving."

He kept his eyes on the ceiling. He couldn't stand to see the disappointment and pity he knew would be in her eyes. "I got a few months of community service, but he got a lifetime of broken dreams."

"Tammy mentioned a wheelchair. He was paralyzed?"

Jake shook his head. "No, his leg was crushed. For about a year he was in a wheelchair, but then he was able to walk after that." He finally looked at her. "But he could never play baseball again."

"So you did it for him."

Jake snorted. "Let's don't make it sound as if I made some kind of noble sacrifice. I was a drunk driver, Brandi. One of those people everyone despises."

"Jake, everyone makes mistakes. You were how old? Nineteen?" Brandi rubbed his arm lightly.

He nodded. "I know that. Believe me, I've repeated it to myself often enough. And I don't struggle with guilt anymore.

I did a terrible thing, but I know I'm forgiven."

"Then why are you still trying to make it right?"

"That's the least I can do. I've tried to make him take half of my baseball income, but he would only take enough to start up his company. Now that it's going strong he refuses my money. So I'm using it to stop something like this from happening again to other people."

"That's noble, but surely you've done enough."

"There is no enough." He spat out the word. "This isn't an abstract hypothetical situation, Brandi. Steve and Elizabeth have to live with my mistake every day. Why shouldn't I?"

"Steve and Elizabeth?" She dropped her hand from his arm and gave him a questioning look.

His ears grew hot. "Steve was my buddy who played first base. He had a surefire major-league career and a beautiful carefree fiancée. But I took him out, got us drunk, and wrapped my truck around a tree. Elizabeth ended up with her groom wheeling down the aisle." His heart ached at the memory. "Knowing how much you like Elizabeth, I hated for you to know I was responsible for the death of her husband's dream."

"That's awful, Jake." Brandi shook her head, but he didn't see the expected disgust in her eyes. "But you have to let it go. Don't Steve and Elizabeth think so?"

"They do. But it's not up to them. Here's the bottom line. If I don't keep on doing what I'm doing, I can't live with myself."

Brandi pushed to her feet. "Everyone has to do what they feel they have to, Jake."

"Brandi?" He stood and touched her arm.

"Yeah?"

"Thanks for not hating me."

She frowned but allowed him to pull her close. "I could never hate you."

He held her tightly in his arms and wished this moment could last forever. But he knew it couldn't. "I'm heading to St. Louis next week for my appointment with the team doctor."

Brandi nodded.

"If things go as I expect they will, they'll approve me to go back into training for next season. I'll sign a new five-year contract before Christmas."

Even in the dim light he could see tears edging her eyes.

He caressed her cheek with his thumb. The idea of not seeing her every day made his heart feel as if it were shattering into a million pieces. "I know I offered before, but I have to try again. We would have houses wherever you want, Brandi. And I'd be home as often as I could."

She shook her head. "I can't live like that. I'd make you miserable." She tried to smile. "Just ask my parents about the year we moved to Arkansas."

"I have to tell you something then before I go to St. Louis."

"What?" Her voice was thick with tears, and she rested her head against his chest.

"I love you, Brandi Delaney. You're everything I could ever want. But if I give up my responsibility in order to have you, I wouldn't be worthy of you anyway." He breathed in the scent of her shampoo, trying to memorize it.

"I love you, too, Jake."

They stood like that in the darkened room, until she finally pulled back. "We'd better get some sleep."

Fat chance. He nodded.

" 'Bye, Jake." She dropped a kiss on his cheek and hurried from the room.

❧

Every mile Brandi drove she wished she were going backward. She pushed herself hard, only stopping for a scant six hours of sleep each night. She tried not to think about the sadness in her parents' voices when she'd called and told them she would be gone before they got home. Or the disappointment evident on her brother's and sisters' faces when they'd realized she was leaving. Most of all she tried not to remember the bereft expression on Jake's face when she'd slipped out of his arms that last night.

Just concentrate on getting home, and everything will be okay.

She pulled into the driveway at about four in the afternoon on the third day of her trip. Without even carrying in her suitcase she stumbled up the stairs to her room and fell into bed.

She didn't have another conscious thought until the doorbell jolted her from sleep. She blinked at the alarm clock—8:00 a.m. She'd promised to call Krista when she made it in.

She grabbed a robe from the rocker at the end of the bed. Funny how she hadn't worn that robe in months, but it had waited for her right there all that time. Why couldn't people be that steady? She stumbled down the hall to the front door and looked through the peephole. Krista wasn't happy she'd forgotten to call.

She threw the deadbolt back and opened the door. "Hi."

"You"—Krista put her hand to her mouth—"look awful."

"Thanks." Brandi hugged her and turned to pad into the living room. She flopped down on the couch.

Krista closed the door and came to sit beside her. "Honey, are you okay?"

"Not really. I think it's jet lag. Only I drove."

"Why were you in such a hurry to get back? It's only December, and you don't have to be back to work until February."

"I missed you?" Brandi squinted at her best friend.

"I missed you, too, but I think there's more to it than that." She pulled her knees to her chest and wrapped her arms around them. "Tell me what's going on."

Brandi laid her head back and poured out the whole story. Her feelings for Jake. His commitment to his cause. Steve and Elizabeth's job offer. What Tammy said at the winter carnival. Jake's reason for playing ball. And finally how Brandi had run away.

"Oh, Bran. What a mess."

"Thanks, but I need something a little more constructive right now." Tears spilled onto her cheeks. She'd cried so much on the trip here that she wondered if her eyes had gotten dry during the night. Or maybe she'd cried in her sleep. It sure felt like it.

"Are you sure you can't travel with him for a few years? He might get tired of it by then."

She shook her head. "Or he might not. And he wants a family. Even though I know she meant it to cause trouble, what Tammy said was right. He's committed to this, and there is no room for compromise with him. I won't go back to the life I had when I was little." She cut her eyes over at her best friend. "You know how I feel about that."

Krista nodded. "Then he's not the man God has in mind for you, Bran."

Brandi shook her head. "No, apparently not, but if we could just let my heart know, that would be great. Maybe we could send a cardio-telegram or something." She tried to laugh, but it turned into a gulping sob.

Krista waited until the sobs quit. When Brandi reached for a tissue, Krista looked at her watch. "I hate to go, but I have to run, or I'm going to be late."

"I know. I'll be fine."

Krista reached out and patted Brandi's hand. "You take it easy today. And tonight, when I get off work, I'm going to take you out to dinner."

"What about Dan?" Krista was normally with her fiancé in the evenings.

"He'll understand. It's girls-only tonight." She smiled. "Be ready at six."

"Okay, I'll be here."

Brandi moped around for a couple of hours after Krista left. The house felt so empty without Gram. And even though it wasn't logical, without Michael, Melissa, and Valerie as well. She'd grown used to their daily presence in her life, and it was going to be harder than she'd thought to go back to seeing them twice a year.

❧

"Michael, hand me that bulb tester again." Jake fought to keep the irritation from his voice. The Delaney kids had all been so down since Brandi left for California that he'd felt compelled to help them put up the Christmas tree.

Unfortunately everything that could have gone wrong had. Two crystal ornaments lay broken on the floor, and each string of lights had at least one bulb burned out. Jake took the tester and worked until he found the guilty culprit.

"I wish Brandi were here." Melissa handed Valerie a gingerbread ornament.

"Yeah—me, too, squirt. But she's not." Valerie ruffled her sister's hair.

Pain stabbed through Jake. How was he going to make it without her? He'd been asking himself that question every day during the week she'd been gone.

"It's not like she's ever been here to help us put up our tree before," Michael pointed out.

"I know," Melissa said. "But I was hoping she'd miss us so much she'd come back."

Valerie nodded. In his heart Jake agreed, but he knew it was an impossible dream. "Okay, that's the last string of lights.

Y'all want to turn them on and try them out?"

Michael hurried to flip the switch, and they all admired their handiwork. Jake was thankful no one mentioned Brandi again.

❧

"So what did you do today?" Krista asked a shade too brightly.

"Not much really today. Mostly I rested."

"Oh, Bran. Couldn't you at least go to the mall? You never get out of the house anymore."

"Yeah, I'm about to change that."

"Really?"

"Yep. I'm going to walk down to the beach tomorrow."

"Well, that's a start."

"Did I tell you Gram called today?" Brandi forced her voice to sound casual.

"No." Krista drew her eyebrows together. "What did she say?"

Brandi picked up their takeout boxes from the coffee table and set on the counter. "Jake got a clean bill of health from the team doc. He's ready to play ball again." She felt tears fill her eyes, so she kept her back to Krista.

She heard Krista clear her throat. "Okay, here's the deal." Even without looking she knew Krista was holding out her hands expressively. "If I don't tell you this, I'm afraid I'll always regret it. And you know my motto is *no regrets*, so I'm going to jump right in."

Krista's laugh was nervous, so Brandi braced herself.

"Bran, you have the strongest faith of anyone I know. But in this one thing you're not seeing it clearly. Instead you're letting your childhood insecurities cheat you out of happiness. 'Home is where the heart is' isn't just a popular catch phrase. Look at you." She pointed at Brandi's pizza-stained sweatshirt. "You don't even care enough to take a shower." Krista's face flamed. "I'm sorry. But think about it. Where is your heart?"

Even though Brandi still felt that her friend didn't really understand her need to have a home, she hated to see her feeling bad. "I promise I'll think about what you said. But, Kris? I don't need a baby-sitter anymore. Five out of the seven nights since I've been back you've ditched Dan for me."

"Dan understands. If the shoe were on the other foot, he'd want you to do the same for me."

"I appreciate both of you. And the Chinese takeout."

"Anytime."

"No. Not anytime." Brandi didn't want to see Krista mess up a good thing on her behalf. "Tomorrow night go out with Dan."

Krista smiled. "Okay, it's a deal."

She walked to the door then turned back. "You could go with Dan and me?"

Brandi gave her a wry grin. "I don't think so."

"Have it your way, but no matter what you decide about what I said, you have to do one thing for me."

"What?"

"You can't keep watching the sports channel 24/7 hoping to see Jake. Give it a rest. Turn it off. Okay?"

"We'll see." Brandi pushed her friend gently out the door.

nineteen

Jake pulled into Steve and Elizabeth's driveway. He'd been surprised when Elizabeth called and insisted he come over tonight. She knew how badly he missed Brandi. Surely she wouldn't try to fix him up on another blind date so quickly. Or ever—after the last time.

He paused on the sidewalk to take in the complete picture. Twinkling icicle lights strung along the rooftop and the Christmas tree in the floor-to-ceiling bay window gave their house a magical feeling. Like nothing bad could ever have happened to the people who lived here. Except he knew better.

"Jake! Come in!" Steve opened the door before he could ring the doorbell. "I'm so glad you came."

He started to shake Steve's hand, but his friend embraced him warmly.

"Elizabeth said it was important."

Steve grinned. "Have you had supper? Elizabeth made a delicious casserole. We have plenty left."

"Thanks, but I ate at the B&B." Jake followed him into the living room. "So where's Elizabeth?"

"She'll be right here."

As soon as the words were out of his mouth, Elizabeth appeared in the doorway.

"Jake! I'm glad you came."

Why did they both say that? Since they'd been friends as long as they had, he hadn't thought he had a choice. He certainly hadn't felt like socializing with anyone, but she'd made it sound like life or death on the phone. He nodded. "I'm afraid I'm not much fun these days."

Steve and Elizabeth exchanged a secret grin. "Well, it's time for that to change," Elizabeth said. "Steve has something to tell you."

Jake groaned inwardly. This was going to be another talk from Steve about how Jake didn't owe him anything and didn't have to play baseball for him.

"You're about to be a godfather."

Jake's eyes widened. "I'm not even in the mafia." Had Steve lost his mind?

They laughed.

"We're going to have a baby," Elizabeth blurted out.

"And we want you to be his godfather." Steve's smile grew wider, if that was possible.

"His?" Elizabeth asked, hands on her hips. "What about hers?"

Jake looked at Elizabeth. "You're expecting?"

She nodded, smiling through the tears that glistened in her green eyes. "Isn't it great?"

"Yes!" He jumped up and hugged her first and then Steve. "You guys, that's fantastic!"

"We think so." Elizabeth beamed.

"Sit down, Jake. There's something else we have to tell you." Steve pointed at the chair.

He complied, and Steve and Elizabeth sat on the couch, holding hands.

"You sure are bossy tonight. It must be practice for being a dad," Jake teased. "There's more?"

Steve smiled. "This isn't news, but it's still important." He cleared his throat and looked at Elizabeth once more. She nodded as if offering private reassurance. When he looked back at Jake, his face was solemn. "When I was a freshman in college, I thought I knew where my life was going. I was on a fast track to the major league, and nothing short of disaster could stop me."

Jake nodded. Why the history lesson? Jake knew all too well about that year.

"I came home with you that weekend and met Elizabeth and loved her almost immediately. But I was selfish and cocky and very goal-driven. When I asked her to marry me, I told her right up front that I didn't plan to have children. She was as much of a distraction from the game as I ever wanted. More, maybe."

Jake frowned. He hadn't known Steve didn't want children. The man had a huge capacity for love. One that Jake had seen even more since the accident.

"She loved me so much she agreed to marry me anyway. Then the accident happened. I've said this before, and you always ignore me, but I could have just as easily been driving. We were both stupid and made a terrible mistake. But you're the one who's going to end up paying for it for the rest of your life if you don't wake up."

"Me?" Jake snorted. "How can you say that? You're the one who was. . ." His gaze was drawn to Steve's leg.

"Damaged?" Steve smiled. "There's more than one way to be crippled. As I said, Jake, we did a terrible thing. But God took that disobedient act, forgave us for it, and turned it into something good. Only God could do that."

Jake frowned. What was Steve getting at?

Elizabeth bounced forward. "Jake, don't you get it? If Steve had gone on to the majors, more than likely we wouldn't have had kids at all."

Steve nodded. "And as cocky as I was, who knows how I'd

have reacted to the temptations that come with being a hot-shot ballplayer? We might not even still be married." He glanced at Elizabeth and squeezed her hand. "But after what we've been through together, now I can't imagine either of us ever choosing that."

"I'm glad you can see something good out of what I did to you—"

Steve held up his hand. "Did you make me get drunk and hold a gun to my head to make me get in the truck?"

"No."

"Then I'm really tired of hearing about what *you* did to *me*." Steve reached over and patted Jake's forearm. "I know you've meant well, but it's time to let my dream die. God has given me something much, much better."

Jake stared at the carpet, unwilling for his friends to know how emotion clogged his throat at Steve's words. When he looked up, the couple had tears in their eyes.

"Jake," Elizabeth said softly. "You always wanted to be a coach. And I know for a fact the head coach job here at the high school is coming open next year. And there's Brandi to consider now." She smiled when she said her friend's name. "Follow your own dream, Jake. Let God make something good for *you* from your mistake."

Jake regarded them through a film of tears. "Your baby is going to be so blessed to have such wise and wonderful parents."

❧

Brandi used a washcloth to clean her face and splashed water on her bleary eyes. After Krista left last night, Brandi had taken a shower and traded in her sweat suit for a T-shirt that said Beach Bum and a pair of jeans. Then she'd stayed up almost all night praying and thinking about what Krista had said.

She still felt unsettled. When she'd gone to the B&B in August she'd known without a doubt where her home was. But now, a thousand miles from Jake, she realized home was so much more than any one place.

Home could be a crowded pizza parlor, a movie theater, or a family gathering. As she stared at her puffy face in the mirror she answered Krista's question. Her heart was with Jake.

So her home must be, too.

She dropped the cloth in the sink and ran to grab her cordless phone. Her hands trembled as she looked up the number for a real estate agent who attended church with her. She punched in the digits and waited. It took her only a few minutes to tell Sue she wanted to list the house.

By noon a FOR SALE sign stood in the front yard. Brandi sank down on the bar stool with a ham and cheese sandwich. Until now the only food she'd eaten since she'd been here was what Krista brought at night. But suddenly details like eating were important. She needed all her strength for cleaning.

After she ate she pulled her hair up in a bear-claw clip letting the ends stick out. Krista called it her runway model look, but Brandi couldn't clean without doing it. Having her hair out of her face was important to getting the job done.

She tackled the bathrooms first and got them sparkling clean. After both bedrooms were finished she headed to the kitchen. Could it be suppertime already? She grabbed some cereal and milk. No time to fix anything. And corn puffs and milk went well with the sports channel. Looking guiltily over her shoulder she remembered Krista had asked her to turn it off.

But Krista was out with Dan.

On her second bite of cereal the sports channel news anchorman captured her full attention. "In other sports news

St. Louis Cardinals pitcher Jake McFadden, who was expected to announce today that he'd signed a new contract with the Cards, instead had a very different announcement to make. Here's an excerpt from his press conference this morning."

The camera faded to Jake in midsentence: ". . .baseball and my work discouraging teen drug and alcohol use have been my life for so long. I thank God for blessing me with success in both areas."

Jake's smile was filled with peace and hope. Brandi's heart thudded in her ears as he continued. "But now I have a dream for a simpler life, one where I'll still work with teens but on a more personal level. I won't be signing a contract with the Cards, and I'm retiring from major-league baseball."

"Mr. McFadden! Mr. McFadden!" Reporters called from all corners of the room.

The picture cut back to the anchorman who looked mournfully at the camera. "It's a sad day in Mudville when Jake McFadden gives up the mound. Jake refused to answer any questions regarding his decision, but he assured reporters it is final, and he's looking forward to a future following his new dream."

Brandi stared at the screen in disbelief then realized she had a spoonful of corn puffs halfway to her mouth. She dropped it back into her bowl and jumped up. She had to— what? What did she have to do? Pack? Turn cartwheels? Run out in the street and yell, "I love Jake McFadden, and I'm ninety-nine percent sure he loves me, too!" at the top of her lungs?

The doorbell rang, and she shoved the bowl onto the counter, heedless of the milk dripping down the sides. She skipped down the hall to the door. "Krista, you weren't supposed to come tonight, you silly goose! But you'll never guess what just—" She looked out the peephole, and the words stuck in her throat. Jake. Jake was on her porch.

She looked down at her housecleaning clothes for a split second then yanked the door open.

He was leaning against the porch post, and she stared at his face, trying to read his mind. For once she was speechless.

"Of all the B&Bs in all the towns in all the world she walks into mine."

Brandi burst out laughing then ran out the door and into his open arms. He swung her around but released her sooner than she wanted him to.

"Brandi, I need to tell you something. I've quit—"

"I know! I saw the press conference a few minutes ago." Tears started streaming down her cheeks faster than she could wipe them off while she was talking. "Jake, I put the house up for sale this morning. I was coming to find you."

He pulled her to him again and wiped her tears with his hand. "You're incredible—did you know that?"

She shook her head. The tender expression in his eyes made her feel like a princess in a fairy tale. The happily-ever-after variety, not the locked-in-tower kind. At least not anymore. "I missed you."

"I missed you, too, honey." He tugged her over to the wicker bench beside the door. She sat down, but instead of sitting beside her he got onto one knee.

"Jake?"

He gently took her trembling hand in his. "Brandi, we can live anywhere you want to live now. I love you more than words can possibly express. Will you please make my dreams come true by agreeing to be my wife?"

"Yes!" she yelled then slapped her hand to her mouth. Leave it to her to make her husband-to-be deaf in one ear before the wedding. "I love you, too, and I don't care where we live."

Jake stood and pulled her to her feet. He lowered his mouth to hers and kissed her soundly. Any scars that lingered on her heart from her tumultuous childhood disappeared with that kiss. Nestled in his arms she knew his love had fulfilled her constant longing for home.

epilogue

"Hey, Jake, nice house!" Holt called with a big grin as they walked up the sidewalk.

Brandi laughed. Five months ago Jake's brother and his wife had welcomed them into this same house for Thanksgiving dinner. Now Holt and Megan were on the porch, and Jake and Brandi stood inside playing host and inviting them in to join the rest of the family for Sunday lunch.

Since his brother had been getting ready to put the house up for sale, Jake had bought it for her as a wedding present. She loved everything about it, especially the fact that it held so many childhood memories for Jake. But always present in her mind was the realization that home wasn't inside four walls.

"Brandi! Megan!" Annalisa called from the kitchen. "We need your help!"

She left Jake with the rest of the men and ran into the kitchen, Megan hot on her heels. "What's wrong?"

Gram stood beside Brandi's mom and Jake's mom right inside the door. They all three backed into the living room, hands up as if to make it plain they had nothing to do with whatever it was.

Jessa and Annalisa both had something white all over their faces, and they were laughing so hard they could hardly breathe. Brandi looked from one to the other in disbelief.

Megan shook her head. "I don't even want to know how this happened." She grabbed a whipped-topping can from each of their hands and set them on the counter.

They looked at her mock-stern expression and laughed harder holding on to each other. Megan looked over her shoulder at Brandi.

"You can't ever leave these two alone. They're trouble waiting to happen."

Brandi grinned.

"She started it!" Annalisa protested, smiling.

"No way!" Jessa got a paper towel and started to wipe her sister-in-law's face. "I told you it was an accident."

Just then Jake came into the kitchen and stopped beside Brandi. Both of the cream-covered women started giggling again. Megan took their arms. "Come on, ladies. We don't want Brandi's new husband to think we're going to corrupt her."

After Megan took them down the hall to the bathroom to get cleaned up, Jake looked over at Brandi. "And you feel at home here?"

She smiled and wrapped her arms around his waist. "Definitely."

A Letter To Our Readers

Dear Reader:

In order that we might better contribute to your reading enjoyment, we would appreciate your taking a few minutes to respond to the following questions. We welcome your comments and read each form and letter we receive. When completed, please return to the following:

Fiction Editor
Heartsong Presents
PO Box 719
Uhrichsville, Ohio 44683

1. Did you enjoy reading *Longing for Home* by Christine Lynxwiller?
   ❑ Very much! I would like to see more books by this author!
   ❑ Moderately. I would have enjoyed it more if

   _____

   _____

   _____

2. Are you a member of **Heartsong Presents**? ❑ Yes ❑ No
   If no, where did you purchase this book? _____

   _____

3. How would you rate, on a scale from 1 (poor) to 5 (superior), the cover design? _____

4. On a scale from 1 (poor) to 10 (superior), please rate the following elements.

   ____ Heroine   ____ Plot
   ____ Hero   ____ Inspirational theme
   ____ Setting   ____ Secondary characters

5. These characters were special because?_____

_____

_____

6. How has this book inspired your life?_____

_____

_____

7. What settings would you like to see covered in future
   Heartsong Presents books? _____

_____

_____

8. What are some inspirational themes you would like to see
   treated in future books? _____

_____

_____

9. Would you be interested in reading other **Heartsong
   Presents** titles? ❑ Yes ❑ No

10. Please check your age range:
    ❑ Under 18   ❑ 18-24
    ❑ 25-34   ❑ 35-45
    ❑ 46-55   ❑ Over 55

Name _____

Occupation _____

Address _____

City_____ State_____ Zip_____

SAN FRANCISCO

4 stories in 1

Four independent women in the San Francisco bay area are about to be swept into a wave of romance.

Letting go to romance will take each woman a step of new faith. Will the arms of love catch them— or will they be shattered by a dream?

Four complete inspirational romance stories by author Kristin Billerbeck.

Contemporary, paperback, 464 pages, 5 ³/₁₆" x 8"

Presents

Great Inspirational Romance at a Great Price!

Heartsong Presents books are inspirational romances in contemporary and historical settings, designed to give you an enjoyable, spirit-lifting reading experience. You can choose wonderfully written titles from some of today's best authors like Hannah Alexander, Andrea Boeshaar, Yvonne Lehman, Tracie Peterson, and many others.

When ordering quantities less than twelve, above titles are $2.97 each.
Not all titles may be available at time of order.

HEARTSONG
P R E S E N T S

If you love Christian romance...

You'll love Heartsong Presents' inspiring and faith-filled romances by today's very best Christian authors...DiAnn Mills, Wanda E. Brunstetter, and Yvonne Lehman, to mention a few!

When you join Heartsong Presents, you'll enjoy 4 brand-new mass market, 176–page books—two contemporary and two historical—that will build you up in your faith when you discover God's role in every relationship you read about!

Imagine...four new romances every four weeks—with men and women like you who long to meet the one God has chosen as the love of their lives...all for the low price of $10.99 postpaid.

To join, simply visit www.heartsong presents.com or complete the coupon below and mail it to the address provided.

$10.99

YES! Sign me up for Heartsong!

NEW MEMBERSHIPS WILL BE SHIPPED IMMEDIATELY!
Send no money now. We'll bill you only $10.99 post-paid with your first shipment of four books. Or for faster action, call 1-740-922-7280.

NAME _____

ADDRESS _____

CITY _____STATE_____ ZIP_____

MAIL TO: HEARTSONG PRESENTS, P.O. Box 721, Uhrichsville, Ohio 44683
or sign-up at WWW.HEARTSONGPRESENTS.COM

ADPG05